The Canyo Gotobed's Overactive Mind

Rob Gotobed

A collection of Rob Gotobed's funniest stand-up routines, articles and social media content from the past thirty years.

This is a work of fiction. Names, characters, businesses, places, events, locales, and incidents are either the products of the author's imagination or used in a fictitious manner. Any resemblance to actual persons, living or dead, or actual events is purely coincidental.

Copyright © Rob Gotobed 2022

All rights reserved. No part of this publication may be reproduced, distributed, or transmitted in any form or by any means, including photocopying, recording, or other electronic or mechanical methods, without the prior written permission of the author or his management, except in the case of brief quotations embodied in critical reviews and certain other non-commercial uses permitted by copyright law.

The right of Rob Gotobed to be identified as author of this work has been asserted in accordance with Section 77 of the Copyright, Designs and Patents Act 1988.

First published in 2022

Cover design by Pieter Kurt Edwards
Book design and production by Richard Castlemaine & Jay Goldston
Editing by Elizabeth Brown
Author photograph on front cover by Pieter Kurt Edwards
All original photographs by Pieter Kurt Edwards

For Julia, Jessica, Pieter & Shaun

Contents

1. The History of Rob Gotobed (Abridged)	1
2. Rob Gotobed's Crazy Pets-R-Me Emporium	9
3. An Exclusive Interview With Rob Gotobed	13
4. Reviews From Rob Gotobed's 2016 American Tour	18
5. Does The Wino Always Sit Next To You?	19
6. Cheese To Replace Oil As A Major Source Of Power	24
7. Inspirational Speeches	26
8. The Principal Causes Of Death In Cricklewood	29
9. The Diary Of Cristiano Ronaldo aged 34¾	30
10. Rob Gotobed's Driving Test	36
11. Rob Gotobed: 22 Things You Never Knew	37
12. The Rob Gotobed Novelty Gift Shop Is Now Online	40
13. Samuel Theakstone	42
14. Did You Know That You Can Set Fire To A Fart?	48
15. The Taxi Driver – A True Story!	54
16. Meanwhile In Another Part Of This Book....	55
17. The Legend of Ricky Slaughter	59
18. How To Make Your Own Pregnancy Testing Kit	64
19. Driving Down To Kraftwerk's Kling Lang Studio	66
20. Rob Gotobed's Christmas Message	72
21. Ugh The Elder's Uprising Against The Romans	78
22. Human Spontaneous Combustion	83
23. MacKing's Burger Drive-Thru Sex Scam	86
24. Rob Gotobed Astrologer Extraordinaire	88
25. Taylor Swift In Rob Gotobed Stalking Shock	94
26. Rob Gotobed: Another 22 Things You Never Knew	97
27. Rob Gotobed's Reversible Toilet Paper	100
28. Gotobed & Knight's Almost Legendary Interview	101
29. Captain Horatio Whiplash And HMS Hesitant	111
30. The Name's Gotobed, Rob Gotobed	116
31. Cricklewood: A Tourist Delight	118
32. Interior: A Boardroom	124
33. Rob Gotobed Campaign For 'Surreal Ale'	129
34. The Tokyo Comedy Store: October 2015	131
35. The Rob Gotobed Stealth Condoms	133

36. American Bald Eagle On American Idol	134
37. Rob Gotobed's Healthy Lifestyle Tips	136
38. Rob Gotobed Inc. Shareholders Annual Report	139
39. Rob Gotobed's Halloween Nightmare	142
40. Rob Gotobed Is Handy Man Extraordinaire	147
41. Fairfield Valley Psychiatric Hospital	153
42. The Legend of King Alf's Camelot	155
43. The Top 116 Favourite Rob Gotobed Tweets	160
44. Rob Gotobed's Almost Legendary Favourite Joke	177
45. Rob Gotobed's Top 30 Favorite Songs About Farting	179
46. My Trip To The Zoo	182
47. Noël Coward's Christmas In Cardiff 1920	190
48. What Scientists Don't Want You To Know	205
49. Jimmy The Sperm	208
50. Rob Gotobed: An Author's Apology 2022	211

51. **BONUS CHAPTER only available to the purchasers of the deluxe, executive version of this book: The complete pilot episode of Rob Gotobed's legendary lost BBC sitcom The Magnificent Moodies!** 214

An Apology

Dear Reader,

Here is an apology.

We apologise most sincerely to those of you who bought this book under the impression that it was in anyway connected with Rob Gotobed.

This was due to an error in the printing stage of the book cover.

This book is in fact called "**The Pyrophone Organ Song Book Of Fish 'n' Ships, Shanties and Sea Songs**." A collection of Old English sea shanties and their translations complied by Horace Titball.

Thank you.

Book cover for The Pyrophone Organ Song Book Of Fish 'n' Ships, Shanties and Sea Songs.

Another Apology

Dear Reader,

On behalf of Rob Gotobed, I would like to apologise for the previous apology. That apology was unnecessary and appeared on the first page of this book due to an administrative error.

This book is NOT, as stated in the previous apology, "**The Pyrophone Organ Song Book Of Fish 'n' Ships, Shanties And Sea Songs**." a collection of Old English sea shanties and their translations complied by Horace Titball but is in fact "**The Canyons Of Rob Gotobed's Overactive Mind**" by Robert 'Isosceles Triangle' Gotobed!

Please accept this, our humblest and only ever so slightly condescending, apology.

Book cover for The Deluxe Executive Version of Rob Gotobed's book.

Welcome And Thank You!

Dear Reader,

Thank you ever so much for purchasing this the Deluxe, Executive version of this Rob Gotobed book. You have chosen wisely, and demonstrated an exemplified taste by agreeing to pay the extra £258.00 for this version of the book.

Each page is so refined, that the top sushi chef from London's Dorchester Hotel has been employed just to slice individual pages from the very best cedar logs that Rob could steal.

The font, although dark in colour is actually **Darth Vader Condensed Extra Bold** and the style of font used is **Stealth Wide Latin Yellow Submarine.** These have been specially hand selected to give you, The Reader, the finest in reading experiences.

The cover has been hand crafted by Little Old Welsh Ladies from specially supplied and dyed Kiwi fruit and the bookmarker is made from the finest kemp.

Unfortunately, if you have purchased the Kindle version of this book you will regrettably have not benefited from any of the above. So in your case this has been a total waste of your time reading this – SORRY!!

And Now A special message from Our Author.

Hi, I'm Rob Gotobed,

Thank you for purchasing this book. How may I direct your eyes across the words?

You know, when I was first asked to express the canyons of my mind to paper I thought blimey, someone's having a laugh?!?!?

But you know, the more I thought of it, I thought "shit" why not! So, here it is.

So, please come with me now and explore the different canyons that make up the Rob Gotobed mind, bagsy first go on the Dumbo ride!

Best wishes

Rob Gotobed

Editor's note: Rob Gotobed is a theme park at the Rob Gotobed World Resort near Orlando in Florida. Owned and operated by The Rob Gotobed Animatronic Company through its Parks, Experiences and Underwear Division, the theme park opened on September 27th 1974.

Rob Gotobed's layout and attractiveness is based in part on the influence of The Goons, Beyond The Fringe and Monty Python.

Rob Gotobed's mind is divided into six themed canyons. They are Main Street Canyon, Adventure Canyon, Frontier Canyon, Liberty Canyon, Fantasy Canyon and Tomorrow Canyon.

Today's opening hours are: 09.00 to 22.00
Extra Magic Time 08.00 to 9.00

Ladies and gentlemen, the Rob Gotobed theme park is now open!

1. The History Of Rob Gotobed (Abridged) Or The Bits He Didn't Want His Fans To Read!

An article of hardly any historical interest as dictated by Robert 'Isosceles-Triangle' Gotobed.

On September 25th 1974 Rob Gotobed was born. He was then born again on the 26th and finally for the last time at 7.30am on the 27th!!

And so the Rob Gotobed story begins at Paddington Hospital, Cricklewood, England, where he immediately demonstrated his independent streak by cutting his own umbilical cord and making a mad dash for the door. Fortunately for us, he was caught and immediately imprisoned in a baby crib.

In 1992 he joined the BBC Radio comedy 'The Rave Show' alongside Rob Brydon and Ruth Jones.

In 1993, Rob gained Scooby Epstein as a manager. So unimpressed was he with Gotobed's style of comedy that he immediately sent him on a tour of the Eastern Bloc. Thinking that the Eastern Bloc was just outside Cricklewood, Rob accepted!

On his return, 'Scooby' put Gotobed into a specialist recording studio which had been built inside a portable chemical toilet. He produced his first comedy album 'What The Hell Just Happened?' in just under 6 minutes. His second, 'Why Do We Have Pubic Hair?' took even longer.

In 2008 'Gotobedmania' hit England. A string of hit comedy shows brought unprecedented scenes of mass ovulation all over the United Kingdom. It seemed that Rob could do no wrong and at one point Rob had nineteen out of the top twenty jokes in the country, even the Queen was a fan, by that we mean Elton John, not the one at Buckingham Palace.

In 2010 the 'Fab One' made the all-important breakthrough in the USA. Ten billion screaming fans were at Los Angeles International Airport to greet him. Unfortunately, Gotobed arrived at the John Wayne Airport.

He was due to be a guest on Conan but as a security precaution he arrived by drone a day early. This enabled him to be safely in and out of the studio before the audience arrived and the show was recorded.

It was a brilliant publicity stunt! The audience were shouting and screaming so hard that the millions watching at home never even noticed that 'Gotobed' didn't even appear on the show. Conan O'Brien described it as the least exciting two minutes of his life.

And now, (F/X Royal Fanfare) we interrupt your reading of this article just so we can annoy you.

Now, back to the story!

***But first a quick recap of what's happened so far......
Britney lay on the bed with just a flower in her hair. "My mother told me to always be good!" she said, "was I?"***

Now back to the real article!

But in the fall of 2011 the 'Fab one' faced the biggest threat to his career. Gotobed in a widely syndicated press interview had apparently claimed that he was now "funnier" than God, and was reported to have gone on to say that God hadn't told a good joke in years.

The story spread like wildfire across the world. Many fans burnt his tweets, although many more burnt their hands attempting to burn his tweets. Gotobed's followers on Twitter skyrocketed. People were following him just to try to burn his tweets. Sales of electronic portable devices also skyrocketed as people burnt them thinking they were burning his tweets.

But in fact it was all an horrendous mistake. Gotobed, talking to an extremely deaf journalist, had claimed only that he was funnier than President Bush.

At a rapidly organised press conference Rob apologised to God, President Bush, Mrs Ethel Picklejar of 25 Ovulation Street, Sidcup, and the press, and so his world tour of 2012 went ahead as planned – but it would be his last!

In 2013, Rob Gotobed faced an even bigger threat to his career when Will Ferrell introduced him to 'Twinkies'.

Gotobed enjoyed the pleasant effects of its creamy fillings, despite warnings that it would lead to stronger things, and it enormously influenced his greatest comedy album, 'Sergeant Gota's Lonely Old Farts Club Twinkie Light Show'.

With such standout tracks as, 'Judy on Sky with James Corden', 'Andy Kaufman's Leaving Home', 'With a Little Help from Dan Aykroyd', 'Lovely Gilda Radner', 'Being For The Benefit of John Belushi' and of course 'A Day with Rob Gotobed's Wife'.

The release of this album – a millstone in comedy history, contributed greatly to an idyllic summer of transcendent sex, incense sticks and Twinkies. But it was not to last. Under questioning Rob refused to lie to the world's press and admitted not only eating and enjoying Twinkies, but '3 Musketeer Bars' and 'Tootsie Rolls' as well, especially the ones with peanut butter.

But as Gotobed sat seeking spiritual enlightenment from Twinkies, fate dealt him an appalling blow. For it was now he learned the shocking news of the loss of his manager Scooby Epstein who had tragically accepted a job with Walmart, working in their frozen fish section.

The news was not a total surprise as Scooby's recent behaviour had been giving Rob grounds for concern. He had recently been filmed filleting fish and there had been rumours of him applying for jobs at Costco and Home Depot to collect shopping carts from the surrounding neighbourhood.

But he had for many years held Rob Gotobed together – often forcibly! Now he was gone, it was the beginning of the end.

In amidst all this controversy Gotobed released his 'I've Arrived! (And To Prove It I'm Not Here)' Album, now famously known worldwide as the 'Beige Album'.

Ambitious in its nature, it has gone down in history as the first comedy album to contain no jokes! In fact the album consists of two sides of silence apart from a very large belch 0.02 seconds from the end of the record. Although, it is rumoured that if you play the belch backwards it says, "I hate peanut butter, honest! And here is the pin number to my bank account."

Meanwhile, Rob had hidden from the public so much that in 2015 a rumour went around that he was dead. He was supposed to have died in a freak accident involving a wishing well and been replaced by a full-size replica of Gus Honeybun.

Several so-called 'facts' helped the emergence of this conspiracy theory. Firstly, on the cover of his latest comedy album he was wearing no trousers or underwear, an old Aztec custom of indicating death. Secondly, Rob allegedly says 'I am dead and buried in Justin Bieber's garden' when you repeatedly play the last track on his Sgt Gota album backwards – in fact he says "Oes gennych chi ddyfais arnofio bersonol!!" Which is very bad Welsh for "Do you have a personal flotation device?"

Thirdly, on the posters for The Gotobed World Tour of 2012, Gotobed is leaning in the exact position of a pregnant llama (From The Rob Gotobed Book of the Unmarried). And finally, if you say the title of 'Sergeant Gota's Lonely Old Farts Club Twinkie Light Show' backwards, it is supposed to sound like 'Rob Gotobed died in December 2011.' In fact it sounds uncannily like "Wohs thgil eikniwt bulc straf dlo ylenol satog tnaegres".

Gotobed was, of course, far from dead. Although not far from Cricklewood. He had fallen into bed with a large-breasted, East German Fräulein called Titania whose father ran the Berlin branch of the H. R. Pufnstuf fan club.

Together they then spent a year in bed as a protest against the planned Cricklewood flyover.

In the midst of this bed-in Gotobed released 'Shit Happens!' as a film, a download, and a lawsuit. The documentary showed Rob Gotobed as never before – bald, web-footed, fatigued, irritable, tetchy and bad-tempered. Gone forever was the image of the happy 'Brazilian-bushed' youngster who had set the world a-laughing.

Then, finally in December 2015 Rob accidentally impregnated himself, three times.

I asked Adam Sandler, 'why do you think Rob Gotobed broke up?'
He said, "Twinkies!" So then I asked Adam 'Do you think Rob will ever get back together again?' He replied, "I hope not!!"

But then miraculously, in mid 2016 from the ashes via Twitter, Rob Gotobed reformed and once again started from rock bottom to create the most spectacular comedy the world would never want to see.....

The End.

**Please note: The Rob Gotobed Archaeology Cds 1,2 & 14 featuring jokes with different punch lines, (and some even with no punch lines at all), outtakes, and the almost legendary lost comedy album, 'Smile You're At Shabby Road Studio' is still available for export on the Apple Tart LP: PCS #7088.

"I'm getting confused, so what you're telling me is that the North Korean leader Kim Jong-Un is not the guy singing Gangnam Style?"

2. Rob Gotobed's Crazy Pets-R-Me Emporium!

Hi, I'm Rob Gotobed and this week I am proud to announce that my new 'Crazy Pets-R-Me Emporium' is now open for business!

Yes, my Crazy Pets-R-Me Emporium offers:

The world's wackiest experiences for pets
We specialise in pet parties, weddings, bar mitzvahs and circumcisions
Kids love it
Leaves adults confused and in need of a lie down

At the Rob Gotobed Crazy Pets-R-Me Emporium® we offer no fuss, just pet accessories, cages and habitats. "*Is there anything else?*" We hear you cry.

No, just pet accessories, cages and habitats.

"But do you sell pets in military tanks?" We hear someone ask.
No you Tosser, it's just pet accessories, cages and habitats.

New for 2022:
Why buy an expensive pet habitat, when you can now hire one of our mobile pet habitats for half the price?

Yes, at Rob Gotobed's Crazy Pets-R-Me Emporium® we now offer our new trailer park service, where instead of purchasing a static pet habitat, you can now rent a mobile pet habitat at one of our conveniently situated pet trailer parks!

You see, over the last two decades, we at Rob Gotobed's Crazy Pets-R-Me Emporium® have secretly been buying up dilapidated trailer parks, whose stereotypical association with peeling paint and unemployed seniors is outdated and been reinventing them as mobile pet home communities, which we saw as a lucrative opportunity to provide housing to low-income American pets.

What's that you say, do we have nostalgic pet habitats otherwise called retro living modules?

Hell yeah! We have pet habitats that remind you of a

gentler age, including 'Victorian Wooden Amusement Park Habitats' which are our speciality.

These Victorian Wooden Amusement Park Habitats include a wooden roller coaster, a bungee rocket catapult ride, and everything from multiple transport tubes to move around in, to a Ferris wheel and even a Haunted Mansion hideout for your pet to enjoy. *(Warning: This product is non-transparent and has a tendency to spontaneously combust within the first two hours of use).*

What about pets that have broken the law and need somewhere to hide out for a while? We hear you exclaim!

Then you need our exclusive gangster's paradise pet habitat!

Yes, our gangster's paradise pet habitat comes with tinted black windows, which is also great for ugly pets, and has bullet-proof glass which can withstand up to two hundred bullets.

How do we come up with these ideas? Rob Gotobed is crazy, that's how!

Would you like a pet habitat for a surfing pet? What about a pet habitat for a poodle who's about to become a nun? Or, what about a nuclear pet submarine habitat for eight cats who want to join the navy? - Well, we've got them all!!!!

How do we stay in business?
Don't you worry about that, Rob Gotobed will worry about that because that's his lookout!!

So, why not come around and ask for me, Mental Rob Gotobed! Or for one of my assistants, Mental Jim Truck-Tucker or Mental Shelia Binliner? We're all mental, and we're ready to serve you!!

Public Notice: Last week's 'Lucky Number' was Pet Habitat Number 78!!

"The world of pet habitats is now a lot safer than it was when I first became President. Advances in pet habitat technology by Rob Gotobed has revolutionised the industry." President Trump The White House July 2020.

"Just tried to share a pizza with a homeless guy I saw sitting in the park. He told me to get lost and buy my own!"

3. An Exclusive Interview With Robert 'Isosceles Triangle' Gotobed by Izzy Ferrari

I was two hours and forty three seconds late for my meeting with Rob Gotobed, according to Mr Gotobed's Head of Security.

I had made arrangements with Irma Bunt, the ex-villainess from 'On Her Majesty's Secret Service', who is now employed as RG's personal secretary, to meet with Rob in his elegant London penthouse suite, but I hadn't banked on the over zealous bodyguards that awaited me.

I had experienced a measure of difficulty before I was actually allowed onto the doorstep. The man in charge of the squad holding the crowds of young women at bay refused to believe that I was there on business, and it was only when Irma phoned down from the penthouse suite to confirm that I had an appointment with Rob that I was allowed in.

After the noise and heat of the street, the Grand Hall was a haven of peace and tranquillity. As my eyes became accustomed to the hideous and garish colour scheme, I saw some of the trappings with which a fantastically successful comedian surrounds himself.

In a corner of the vast hall was a German Panzer tank, on which generations of fans had scrawled their phone numbers in a bewildering variety of cheap lipsticks.

On the wall was a range of fine paintings. I recognised an early Justin Bieber, two de Paris Hilton's and at least five efforts in crayon by Lady Gaga. There was also a full-sized map of Katy Perry and several posters advertising Rob's sensational gigs in places as far apart as the top of Shaftesbury Avenue and the bottom of Shaftesbury Avenue.

An Exclusive picture of the only chair Rob Gotobed sits in while using the internet.

I was then left to fester in this unattractive, environmental disaster for six hours as Rob watched re-runs of the I Love Gotobed Show.

Regrettably, Rob does not believe in chairs and there were none in sight, so I spent most of the time leaning up against an unattractive wall painting by Franz Schubert.

Now, Schubert might have been a great composer but he was a God-awful painter.

Finally, Irma, a stunningly unattractive ex-Smersh Assassin with a Russian styled hairstyle wearing a grey suit of matching ugliness, came down to tell me that I could now go up to the bathroom and fix the blockage in the toilet.

I explained that I had been sent by The Los Angeles Journal to interview Rob and to discover his feelings on the seventies craze of Cabbage Patch Dolls. She laughed in a sinister way and disappeared upstairs again.

Forty two minutes later she reappeared as ugly as ever, and told me that Monsieur Gotobed would see me now. The elevator did not seem to be working, so Irma and I walked up the thirty-eight flights of stairs to Rob's private suite.

In between gasping for breath I asked her what it was like to work for such a creative genius? Was it true, I wanted to know, that he was making a new comedy film based on the components of the internal combustion engine?

Had he, I wondered, really severed his relationship with the glamorous starlet Emily Shagherharder - who reacted to Rob breaking off their passionate love affair by turning to lesbianism? Irma passed me a water melon from a bowl on the staircase but made no answer.

From time to time as we climbed the numerous sets of stairs I saw the shadowy and scantily dressed figures of thirty-something young women of all hues and nationalities flitting in and, indeed, out of such rooms as The Picture Gallery, with its unique collection of rare illuminated medieval codpieces, The Blue Drawing Room, with its teak-panelled sauna and spa recreation centre for the exhausted comedian, the Jester's Gallery, with an extensive full-scale replica of the Paris Metro system, and the private zoo, in which Rob keeps the three snow leopards he takes with him whenever he tours the comedy clubs of North America.

Rob Gotobed during his 2002 tour of Australia.

Eventually Irma and I reached the great man's lair and were ushered in by two scantily dressed female stormtroopers, who come, I believe, from Chattanooga City in Tennessee.

Rob was already up when I walked into the room, (a problem Rob regularly suffers from first thing in the morning) and one of the girls in the room offered me a Gotobed Sunrise. I accepted gratefully and handed her the nutritious water melon Irma had given me earlier.

Rob beckoned me over to the full size replica of New York's NoMad bar next to his Baldacchino Bed. He then motioned me on to a Victorian bucking-bronco rocking horse, and asked me to remove all clothing in case of accidents.

He then clambered back into his bed, where a furtive giggle came from what I had hitherto supposed to be a heap of clothing on the pillows. Then having made my apologies for being so late, I began the interview....

Interview by Izzy Ferrari.

"Hi, I'm Rob Gotobed, hope you are too!"

"Sad to think, that I've accomplished far more in playing ten minutes of "Fortnite" than I have in my entire real life up to now!"

4. Some Of The More Flattering Reviews From The Opening Night Of Rob Gotobed's 2016 American Stand-Up Tour

"I don't think legally this qualifies as comedy!" ***Kathy Brûlée*, Time In Magazine.**

"An absolutely horrible show. It was opening night of his stand-up tour and Rob Gotobed was already using an understudy" ***Izzy Ferrari*, Los Angeles Entertainment Journal.**

"The only time the audience applauded was when I threw a shoe at his head" ***Zach O'Brian*, The Chicago Beano.**

"It's the most upsetting experience I've ever had in a comedy club" ***Benjamin T J Hooker*, The Boston Gazette.**

"Phew! Better than expected!" ***Rob Gotobed*, Fall 2016**

"Just been reliably informed by Royal Mail that the letterbox on your front door is so that you can tell your postman you love him!"

5. Does The Wino Always Sit Next To You On The Subway?

When you're riding on the subway, does the Wino always sit next to you? Because the Wino always sits next to me!

It doesn't matter how many people are on the train the Wino always manages to spot me, waves to me likes he's known me for years and comes over and sits right next to me. It doesn't matter if I'm the only one on the train once he's spotted me over he comes.

For the life of me I can't understand why? I'm just sitting there, minding my own business, and the train stops, the only people in my carriage get off, nobody gets on, and the train starts off again. Then suddenly I turn around, and from out of nowhere, there's a wino in my face.

"Hey buddy, is this seat next to you taken?" I always hesitate with my reply "Ah, yes…. Yes it is". To which the Wino always replies, "Yep, I thought not". And then, he just plonks himself down right next to me.

I think there must be an invisible sign above my head which reads "Wino Lover" which only Winos can see.

Of course, once he's sat next to me, anyone and everyone on the subway can enjoy the show! You even see the train driver give a noticeable sigh of relief! "Woh, thought I was going to be the one stuck with the Wino there for a moment."

And why do Winos love to show you things? Because Winos always love to show me things.

Wino: I've got an umbrella here that once belonged to Abraham Lincoln!

Rob: Oh right, that's nice.

Wino: No, it's not! It hasn't got any canopy. It's just made up of these metal ribs.

Rob: Well, that won't keep you dry.

Wino: I don't use it for that. I use it to contact UFO's!

At which point the Wino takes off his 1982 World Series baseball cap to reveal a head wrapped in Aluminium foil.

Rob: What's that for?

Wino: To stop the aliens from lasering my brain.

Rob: I would have thought they were too late.

Wino: What? What? ....Do you know what the best advice I ever got was?

Rob: No.

Wino: "Look out!"

The Wino then begins to laugh uncontrollably at his own joke.

Rob: I don't believe in any of this UFO stuff. I'll only believe it when I see an alien for myself.

Wino: Well, here's a thought for you then Mr High 'n' Mighty, what if aliens do come here all the time, but secretly they are really shy and just want us to make the first move. Have you ever thought about that?

Rob: Look, if aliens do ever invade our planet, the first question they'll have is, why does Kermit the Frog's voice keep changing so much when all the other Muppets voices stay the same?

Wino: Anyway, I know for a fact that we've already made contact with the aliens and they're way cooler than us! For example, they had a different shaped fender on their 1959 Chevy Impala bubble top car and they can surf forever without falling off their surfboards.

Rob: Oh right!?!?

Wino: Anyway, none of this really matters!

Rob: Why not?

Wino: Because, we're all probably going to die fighting for food and batteries after the apocalypse. ....By the way, have you paid your fare?

Rob: Yes.

Wino: Where's your ticket then?

Rob: Here!

The Wino then grabs hold of my ticket rips it up and throws the pieces up in the air.

Wino: Rip, rip rip! Oh look, I've made some confetti! I love weddings, do you love weddings?

Rob: No, not particularly.

Wino: Oh, I love them! Mind you, I've never been the best man at a wedding. ……But I've been the worst man at almost all of them!!

The Wino then punches me in the stomach and begins to laugh uncontrollably at his own joke.

Wino: Anyway, no man should ever be nervous about getting married. The reality is, that 86% of it is just pretending to be excited when the new cooker arrives.

Rob: I have a question for you? Why do they call people like you winos? Is it because you love wine?

Wino: Well friend, I'm glad you asked me that. You see, the word "Wino" originated in the USA around 1910, when a popular form of slang at the time was to take a word and add an 'o' to the end of it to describe a person.

Rob: I did not know that.

Wino: Yes, it is true. In fact, I don't even like the stuff, but my girlfriend has got an excellent nose for wine.

Rob: Really?

Wino: Yep, it's shaped like a corkscrew!

The Wino once again punches me in the stomach and begins to laugh uncontrollably at his own joke.

But I'll tell you what the main problem is with a Wino on the subway. It's that they'll never let you get off.

I once spent two weeks on the subway with a Wino!

The lost black and white classic Ingmar Bergman film, "The Seventh Muppet" has recently been restored and remastered. The film depicts the violence and the struggle of modern life through a game of chess played between a disillusioned Kermit The Frog and the figure of Death.

6. Professor Rob Gotobed's World Exclusive: Cheese To Replace Oil As The World's Major Source Of Power

"Yes I believe that cheese power is something we must look at seriously. Not only is cheese clean and environmentally-friendly, it also comes in hundreds of different varieties including sheep, goat, buffalo and ant" claimed Professor Rob Gotobed yesterday from the steps of **The Golden Statue of Poseidon** located in **The Lost City of Atlantis**.

"What I predict", Prof. Gotobed said, "is that filthy coal burning power stations and dangerous nuclear reactors will vanish from our countryside, to be replaced by huge cheese powered windmills, and huge cheese powered turbines along the coast!!!"

Prof. Goodinbed also went on to state that gas and petrol pumps would be replaced by giant cheese-boards and that cheese driven cars will be cleaner, faster and safer to drive.

He also said that "the overall savings and benefits to the aviation industry would far out way the fact, that in the future, all aeroplanes would need to be wrapped first in parchment or waxed paper, and then loosely covered in plastic wrap or a plastic baggie!"

He did reluctantly admit to one downside, that the likely cost of converting your average 5 passenger SUV would be somewhere in the region of $2.4 million!!

I demanded of Prof. Gotosleep that this was just some cheap publicity stunt to publicise his latest show 'The Complete & Utter History of Rob Gotobed's Tool Shed' due to tour in the Fall of 2020.

Only this week the show received a new sponsor, America's Cheese Marketing Board!! "Nonsense" replied Prof Gototown, as he offered me another cheese toastie! "I like cheese, some of my best friends are made of cheese and my first real girlfriend was called, Cheesy Williams! - So stick that in your sandwich with some onions and smoke it!!"

Please note: Rob Gotobed's unique range of home-brewed cheeses are now available from his online shop. They include Lancashire Hop Cheese, Sheep Dip Surprise,* Sergeant *Gota's Stinking Archbishop and Stiffy's Delight!

"Honestly, you don't really get the total experience of the Harrods escalator unless you put your hands in the air & scream all the way down!"

7. Inspirational Speeches

And now another in our series of 'How To Give An Inspirational Speech'.

Number 86 - In The Soccer Dressing Room.

Right lads, thanks for all the congratulations for scoring 50 goals in the first half, it really does mean a lot to me.

You know, whether I'm chasing a goal scoring record or playing a dangerous game like Assassin's Creed or Fortnite, people ask if I get scared? But honestly I can say "no", your training just takes over.

But I'd like to take this opportunity to thank some of the lads in the team; Pound Sterling, Oxymoron and of course, Tony Hart in goal. Not forgetting our manager Roger Hodgson who has had a lot of success himself since he left the rock band Supertramp.

You know, as a child, a lot of people told me that watching 'The Flintstones' gave me unrealistic expectations for the future. Like, having a wife who loves me and owning a dinosaur. .....But how wrong were they, right?

Another thing I really miss from my childhood is how much more freedom you had to throw bricks at people. But probably best to save that for another occasion.

Also, I find it really heartbreaking to think that although most ordinary adults will go their entire lives without ever having the opportunity to travel to another time dimension and to investigate a distress signal from a seemingly deserted space station, I did, so that's great!

You know Alex Ferguson once told me nothing's impossible. Like the time I wanted to buy a koala bear from London Zoo and they wouldn't let me. But I got my own back by duct taping two squirrels together.

It's really weird but about three weeks ago Lionel Messi showed up in my shower, washed my body, and then whispered, "No one will ever believe you." And walked away.

You know a wise man once asked me, "if a Premier League footballer falls over in a forest and no one is there to see it, do they still roll around on the ground acting like their leg exploded?" And the answer is yes, yes they do!

But I guess I still haven't achieved my ultimate dream yet. And that is to have a type of cheese named after me. The Gota! "Can I have another slice of Gota please mum?" Sounds epic doesn't it!

Also, one question still baffles me. Why do hot dogs come in packs of 10, but buns come in packs of 8? Because I eat 18 hot dogs every meal!?!?

And since you asked, nothing makes me feel more insignificant than a public toilet flushing while I'm still sitting on it.

So finally, in conclusion, remember lads that we are all like snowflakes, each one of us is unique, each one of us is original, and a bunch of us together in a bar at the same time is annoying as f**k!

Thank you.

Ronaldo Gotobed

"They say revenge is a dish best served cold! But I like revenge baked at gas mark 6 and have you tried sautéed revenge? OMG try it now!"

8. The Principal Causes Of Death In Cricklewood 2010 – 2020

Rob Gotobed exclusively reveals the principal causes of death in Cricklewood between 2010 – 2020 (Per Person).

Boredom	**170**
Non-voluntary organ donation	**381**
Internet porn addiction	**205**
Internet notification distraction.	**5**
Shot while trying to escape	**2**
Coronary while watching internet porn	**112**
Coronary while taking person to hospital who had coronary from watching internet porn	**214**
Contraceptive overdose	**9**
Fatality at experimental traffic junction	**74**
Dental floss abuse	**3.1**
Relish abuse	**7.2**
Surreal ale addiction	**14**
Posh Spice's new fashion jeans	**19**
Spontaneously Combusted	**8**
Attempting to dunk donuts while having sex	**716**

"Is it just me, or does it feel like you're sleeping with a REAL women just by shaving one of your legs?"

9. The Diary Of Cristiano Ronaldo Aged 34¾

The completely made-up diary of a superstar and a world class footballer - Or is it?!?! Ha ha just joking, no it's not!

MONDAY.
Just read an article that the typical professional footballer's body consists of between 6.1 to 19.5% of fat. Ha!! Ronaldo does not do fat! I spend up to 25 hours a day in the gym. I can do a million squat-thrusts without blinking – by the way that's not my gym routine, that's my sex life!

TUESDAY.
Spent the morning training with the lads at Juventus Football Club. Some people in the world think I've been going downhill since I left Real Madrid, but that's not how I see it! I mean Real Madrid's got a crap shopping centre but here in Turin, Juventus' training ground is near Piazza Gran Madre di Dio. To

me, that's real progress especially with all the Italian designer clothes and quirky furniture shops.

WEDNESDAY.

I am very interested in Italian politics. In fact, I am still furious about the whole Italian government ministers expenses scandal! It's disgusting that some Italian minister is claiming expenses for his moat! I am really outraged! How come he's got a moat and I haven't! I've got the diggers coming to our castle next Monday.

THURSDAY.

My Georgina is in a proper strop all because she caught me chatting up another woman! I told her we were debating farm subsidies in the European Economic Area. She immediately picked up a frying pan and said, "Oh yeah? Well debate this!!"
She then hit me over the head three or four times with the frying pan. I'm not really sure how many times, because you don't really count, do you? I must admit though, I don't remember much after the second whack!

FRIDAY.
Memo to legal team, reference my purchase of new $81 million New York penthouse on Park Avenue. I have read the surveyor's report saying that a subway runs beneath the penthouse block and that it may cause some slight noise. Please can you call the Mayor of New York and order him to move subway!! Thank you x

SATURDAY.
Played a football match, then took Georgina out to dinner to make up for our fight on Thursday. Obviously, I got a little bit confused and when I thought I was ordering Rocky Mountain Oysters, we got served a mixture of bull and sheep testicles instead. But living in all these different places, it takes a lot to get used to all the new kinds of food. But Georgina never has any trouble. Like she says, "a testicle is always a testicle, anywhere in the world."

SUNDAY.
Hooray, I can still fit in the same football kit I had

when I was sixteen years old!!

According to the latest figures, I am now worth 480 million dollars, and if you include my girlfriend Georgina's earnings over the same period ....Wow, that's 480 million dollars!!

MONDAY
Diggers arrived today to start work on our moat.

TUESDAY
Work on moat is progressing really well.

WEDNESDAY
I've got a moat!

THURSDAY.
Went to visit Lionel Messi. It was a total nightmare!! All he ever wants to do is play me on Just Dance 2019, I don't mind because I always win. But what really bothers me is that he won't stop playing One Direction's albums all the time.

So, okay, their debut album *'Up All Night'* is okay, but 'Made in the A.M' come on, really Messi? The production on that album is all over the place, it lacks substance and there's no use of the bass as a musical counterpoint!?!?

Worst of all, he sings like a strangled cat!!

FRIDAY.
Disaster! Couldn't wash my hair this morning, because Georgina has decided that shampoo gives you cancer and has thrown all of my bottles out of the house. 'Forget cancer', I shouted! 'I need shine and volume now, Bitch!!!'

SATURDAY.
I am displeased by the behaviour of Luka Modrić, Gareth Bale, Kylian Mbappé and Neymar Jr. all of who have been getting more media coverage than me recently! All of this could conceivably make me unhappy. But this cannot be allowed. Ronaldo does not do 'unhappy!!'

This afternoon I scored another hat-trick for Juventus against Atlético Madrid, and this time I wasn't even wearing my lucky thong! Oh well, time to unwind and watch my favourite episode of In The Night Garden. That Igglepiggle really cracks me up, especially when he keeps leading Upsy Daisy on. Man, she is so stupid, she doesn't even realise that he's never going to marry her.

Mind you, I'm not the brightest spark in the firework display. I remember telling Georgina once that I thought Makka Pakka was an old team mate of mine from Manchester United.

Goodnight everyone.

Go to sleep Tombliboos, and go to sleep Lionel Messi.

"After the Bond films the number of babies named Blofeld dropped dramatically!"

10. Rob Gotobed's Driving Test.

I was always told that on a driving test that if an animal steps out in front of your car, you should always run it over. This is because swerving could potentially be dangerous to other road users and even though no one wants to kill an animal, drivers must realize that their own life and safety is more valuable than that of an animal.

Well, on my driving test, a giraffe stepped out in front of my car!

I know, a bloody giraffe, what are the chances of that happening? Apparently, someone had left their garden gate open and the giraffe just sneaked out

So, as I went past him, I nervously looked in my rear view mirror. The giraffe was fine. I had missed him by millimetres.

Now, obviously, I didn't want to fail my test, so I slapped the car into reverse and drove after the giraffe.

I must have been chasing that bloody animal all over Cricklewood for a good half an hour before I finally hit him!

And my driving examiner still failed me!!

"I call my girlfriend's boobs "Simon & Garfunkel" because they're both different and one is slightly smaller and weirder than the other one!"

11. Rob Gotobed: 22 Things You Never Knew!

1. Rob Gotobed is not the Rob Gotobed mentioned in the bible.

2. Every night Rob goes to sleep with both middle fingers sticking up just in case a burglar breaks in during the night.

3. Rob Gotobed thought he once heard a Harley-Davidson approaching but it turned out to be 600 bees riding a regular bicycle.

4. Rob's hobby of recreating aerial dogfights is really expensive. He says you're looking at between 90 and 100 helium filled balloons just to lift one poodle.

5. Rob once went into a bank, pulled out a gun, and shouted "Everybody be cool!" ....And then handed out sunglasses and baseball caps.

6. Rob was once shot at by a bank security guard just for pulling out a hair dryer and trying to fix a bank teller's hair.

7. On one occasion Rob successfully breastfed an injured giraffe back to health.

8. Rob was going to go as 'The G Spot' to a Halloween party last year but he couldn't find the costume.

9. To make his pectoral muscles, Madame Tussauds Waxworks in London had to melt down both Justin Bieber AND Lady Gaga.

10. Rob thinks there's no nicer feeling than urinating into a bottle. But other times he hates his part-time job at the brewery.

11. Rob once showed his tattoo of his grandmother to his other grandmother. .....To be honest, it didn't go well.

12. Rob Gotobed once had an affair with Daphne Blake.

13. Rob actually believes that it was Zorro who put the mark on Harry Potter's forehead.

14. Rob's favourite word which he's never actually used is kerfufflepuff.

15. In 2015, he claimed to buy toilet tissue by the grit rating.

16. In 2016, he claimed it was 'he' who took the bite out of the Apple logo.

17. In 2017, his belly button exploded during a live television debate.

18. Many men are intimidated by beautiful women who shoot bolts of lightning from their breasts. Not Rob, he draws them all the time.

19. Some ancient South American tribes believe that if Rob Gotobed should remove his underpants the world will come to an end.

20. In time of war it is against the Geneva convention to have SEX with Rob Gotobed.

21. To this day, Rob still won't reveal which Muppet he dated for seven months in 2012. Our money is on Beaker.

22. Rob Gotobed is not interested in publicity.

NB. All facts were correct at time of going to press.

"I just realised I never said "unquote" after reciting a Mark Twain speech at University. Sorry if you thought everything I've said since is by him!"

12. The Rob Gotobed Novelty Gift Shop Is Now Online!

Hi!

My name is Rob Gotobed and I run The Rob Gotobed Novelty Gift Shop.

People often ask me how I keep my prices so low at The Rob Gotobed Novelty Gift Shop?

Well, my friends, the answer is simple. All my products are stolen goods that I buy from thieves.

I also don't offer a guarantee or after-sales service on any of my products.

I can also assure you that you won't find any quality brands at The Rob Gotobed Novelty Gift Shop, but you will find two large Rottweiler dogs and a M134 Modern Gatling Gun in the yard at the back of the shop. So don't you be getting any "silly" ideas now!

Today's special offer….

The Rob Gotobed 2023 calendar.

One of my happy customers writes…

Dear Rob Gotobed

What a con most of these so-called "calendars" are. Not so, the superb effort from Rob Gotobed which gives us 36 days in July and a whopping 46 days in August!

What a bargain for my $9.99!! Just like Rob Gotobed to give such good value in two months when it's warm enough to enjoy the extra 20 days!!

Good on you Rob!

Love and bear hugs

King Charles III xxx   PS: The Corgi says "Hi!"

"But seriously! She can't really leave you if you're wearing all her underwear? ....Can she?"

13. Samuel Theakstone

Samuel Theakstone, England's most prolific classical composer was born in Cricklewood on May 5th 1857.

Born with an IQ of -5, Theakstone spent the first forty years of his life showing very little sign of the musical talent which in later years was to escalate him to world obscurity.

In fact, during those first forty years he had shown very little sign of life, and several of his most intimate friends and lovers had presumed he had been dead for years.

It is however unfortunate that all of Theakstone's music was left unfinished. As Samuel's wife Alice was to write in her autobiography 'My Life With Nutty Sam!' "If only I could get Samuel to finish one of his compositions, we would be rich! It's like writing a book and not bothering to complete the last page. Most composers leave their work unfinished due to their untimely death, so what's Samuel's excuse? He just thinks it's "hip and cool" to write unfinished music for some unearthly reason."

Although there was a widely reported story that at one

time Theakstone accidentally finished a composition, this was never actually substantiated and the rumoured piece 'Romp and Circumcision March Number One in D Major' has long since disappeared. If indeed it ever did exist.

To gain some inclination from where Theakstone found his inspiration to compose such awful music, you have to appreciate the Cricklewood into which Theakstone was born.

Theakstone was alive during the hey-day of the glorious Cricklewood Empire, where for just 2d he could watch a B movie and a main feature all in one afternoon.

Having achieved very little in the way of composition during 1857, the year of his birth, Theakstone continued this trend until 1877 when he begrudgingly arranged five pieces, including two by Mozart, as studies for the banjo.

But in 1878, Theakstone devoted the year of his twenty-first birthday to the task of teaching himself to be a serious composer.

So why on earth, he enrolled for cookery lessons in London with Adolph Menuhin is a complete mystery! But, during that same year, he managed to unfinish several unfinished Chamber works, an unfinished Fantasia for banjo, piano, strings and saw, and an unfinished Allegro for the kitchen spoon and AGA cooker.

While struggling as a serious composer and part-time cookery student, he decided to subsidise his studies by giving banjo lessons to the people of Cricklewood (whether they wanted them or not is of course another story). But Theakstone was frequently to be seen forcibly giving banjo lessons to unsuspecting victims in dimly lit alleys.

One of these so-called victims was a Mrs Edith Picklejar of no fixed hair-piece, who wrote in her diary of the day, "Mr Theakstone is full of helpful encouragement to the would-be apprentice banjo-player and tonight when I enquired of him about what sort of banjo to purchase? He replied, 'Preferably one with strings on'. Obviously the remark of a genius I would say".

Unfortunately, two months later before she had the chance to master the instrument, she was run over by an escaped tone-deaf, banjo-hating midget riding a horse and carriage.

Arnold Jaguar, Theakstone's publisher at Novello, a widely unrespected musical figure of his day, who was destined to achieve immortality as the 'Flying Sunderland' in Theakstone's 'Enema Variations', was a fanatical enthusiast about Theakstone's work. A typical letter received by Theakstone began:

My Dearest, Darling Samuel,

Your work grows on me with each dying second of the

day. It's great stuff me ol' mate and quite wonderfully original and beautiful!

Bless you, this is your finest work so far, and your greatest! I fear that though God in his infinite wisdom gave me two hands of no artistic merit whatsoever, to group them in the same general term 'hands' which includes yours, is a blasphemy of the worse kind.

I fear that the only action left open to me is to chop them both off and send them to some far off darkened corner of our glorious Empire!

Two weeks later Jaguar's blood stained hands turned up in Daisy Mcdonald's, the apprentice usherette's, confectionery tray at the Cricklewood's Empire cinema.

Thereafter Jaguar dictated all his future correspondence.

In later years over zealous with his fanatical devotion to Theakstone's work, he would immediately rush down from London to give Theakstone vital encouragement and to let him know the precise point at which to leave the piece unfinished.

During this time, Theakstone was rapidly developing a huge cult following. The Cricklewood Chronicle ran a four page feature on him complete with a dozen photographs, all of them carefully posed and with only two full frontal.

The photographs were all designed to show that when at home, great men behave just like anyone else, doing perfectly ordinary things like smoking a kipper, riding a unicycle and composing an unfinished oratorio or two,

Like so many of their contemporaries, the Theakstone's looked ten years older than they were. Samuel had been voting for several years by the time he was eleven and he reached seventy long before his age caught up with him. But when it eventually did, he became extremely erratic and eccentric in his ways.

When his specially commissioned unfinished choral music was to be performed at Westminster Abbey, he became so paranoid about people stealing his creation and actually having the nerve to finish it, that he would only show a few pages of the work to each section of the orchestra.

As the leading music critic of the day wrote in the London Times, "Not only is Samuel Theakstone's music unfinished – but it is also crap as well!"

Heartbroken by this latest panning by the so-called 'music press', deeply distressed by the lack of enthusiasm for any of his life's work and feeling that his life had been a total waste of time, he took his own life in a freak accident involving some hedge shears.

Then in accordance with his last wishes, his ego was donated to The Cricklewood Memorial Hospital's maternity wing.

Many years later, one of England finest unfinished musicians called Benjamin Hill wrote a song in Samuel Theakstone's honour. It ended like this....

"Samuel was only 76, he didn't want to die,
And now he's gone to make unfinished music in the great and heavenly sky.
Where the audience are angels and ferocious critics are banned,
And the composer's life is full of fun in that hairy, fairy land.

But a lustful woman has many needs, and soon Alice she remarried,
But strange things happened on Alice's wedding night as she lay in her bed.
Was that the trees a-swishing? Or the mud flaps on her bike?
Or Samuel's ghostly unfinished Fantasia music, performing from beyond the grave?

No, they won't forget Samuel, (Samueeeeeeeeel!) And he wrote the fastest unfinished oratorio in the West."

"Have you ever noticed how men look at breasts the same way that women look at babies?"

14. Did You Know That You Can Set Fire To A Fart?

Well, did you know that you can set fire to a fart?

You did, good!

Because the reason I ask, is that there are some people who know that you can set light to a fart, and then there's the majority, who don't know that you can set light to a fart!

Yes, the millions of uninitiated people who have never experienced or witnessed someone lighting their farts.

Now this is not a participation sport only for football mad males with high testosterone levels, oh no, I have seen my own fair share of the delicate female sex set their farts alight!

Obviously, we're not talking classy women here, but you would be surprised at the number of female students who after a few drinks too many on a Saturday night can't wait to demonstrate their favourite party trick.

These are what I would call "feisty" women! Now here is a piece of interesting trivia for you, did you know that the original use of the word "feisty" in old English was to describe someone with terrible flatulence.

It's true, if you don't believe me look it up. This is one of the biggest male in-jokes of all time to call a woman "feisty".

Your honour, if it pleases the court, I would like to submit the following phrases for your consideration.

What a feisty woman!
Translation: What a farty woman!

You're a bit feisty tonight darling!
Translation: You're doing a lot of farty chuff-chuffs tonight darling.

No wonder Dame Helen Mirren took umbrage to being told by one particularly uneducated American interviewer that she played a lot of feisty women on the big screen. Anyway, as usual I digress, back to setting light to farts.

Now as you would expect there is a definite art to setting your farts alight! First of all you have to make sure you have eaten plenty of tinned baked beans, or sardines, or had a curry during the day and built up quite an excessive store of gas.

Also, you have to make sure that you have a reliable cigarette lighter with the flame adjusted to the correct setting, otherwise you may well land up with a singed bottom and if you have a particularly hairy posterior you may inadvertently start a 'bush' fire!

Then finally there is the art of getting the timing right, which is, Fart-Click-Light!

If you have never seen someone set light to a fart then I suggest you add it to your bucket list straight away. For in my humble opinion, it is the eighth wonder of the world and definitely on a par with that equally gaseous phenomenon, the aurora borealis, otherwise known as the Northern Lights.

But there is one major draw back that I should make you aware of. It happened to my mate Carl Fisher who had somewhat a heightened reputation for setting his farts alight and would immediately drop his trousers and underwear and demonstrate his prowess at any given opportunity to win a bit of money.

Anyway, this one night we were at a party at a students hall of residence. When suddenly at about 1.00am Carl was persuaded to demonstrate to all those gathered there, that lighting a fart was not only possible, but for the princely sum of £35.00 he would demonstrate it.

To be honest, I have never seen so-called poor students raise £35.00 so quickly. But raise it they did and soon the bet was on!

Everybody at the party gathered in one room, Carl took up his place centre stage, he quickly ate some more sardines just to add to a bit more gas to the furnace.

He then removed his jeans and underpants, lay down on the sofa, raised his legs in the air, put the lighter as near as possible to his Channel Tunnel entrance, let rip a humongous fart and set it alight with the cigarette lighter in his hand.

The flame went approximately three feet and singed a young girl's eyebrows who had ventured too close to view. There was an almighty cheer and everyone applauded.

Then Carl said, "I'm not finished yet" and immediately let out an enormous follow up fart which he mistimed with his lighter!

The result was an horrendous blow-back! Now for anyone who's seen the film Backdraft this phrase needs no explaining! But for those of you who haven't, what it meant was that the flame went backwards instead of forwards!!

Carl was in agony and the little hairs on his singed bum were all alight.

Now obviously, myself and my mates were totally sympathetic, "Shame Carl, that would have been a real good one mate!"

"Shut up!" cried Carl, and "get me to the nearest Accident and Emergency Department!!"

When someone asked why? I will never forget his reply, "Coz the flame's gone up inside my bum hole!!"

Well, my mates and I couldn't stop laughing, but somehow we picked him up quickly and took him to the nearest car with a sober driver and set off for the local hospital.

We'd only gone about ten feet when a policeman pulled us over. Well, eight students in a mini and a singed bum sticking out of the window he had to.

"So, what's happened here lads?" said the policeman.

Then the sober girl who was driving explained what had happened, well the rest of us couldn't because we were all giggling like schoolboys in the back of the car.

The policeman turned out to be very sympathetic and even gave us a police escort to the local hospital complete with flashing blue lights and siren.

But the really magic moment was when we got to the hospital and the policeman met a rather old prim and proper Staff Nurse who was coming out to see what all the commotion was about.

And even before the policeman opened his mouth to tell her what had happened, she had taken one look at the singed bum sticking out of the car window and said in a very posh accent, "Has Carl Fisher been trying to set fire to his farts again?"

"I grew up on a tough British council estate. We had the typical gang. You know, Scarface, Fatso, Rottweiler, Chunkie-Wunkie, Stinky! ....Then there were the boys!!

15. The Taxi Driver – A True Story!

A friend of mine was in a minicab in London when she leaned over and gently tapped the driver on the shoulder.

The cabbie screamed, lost control of the taxi, drove over the kerb onto the pavement and stopped about two inches from a large plate-glass window of a supermarket.

The taxi driver said, "I'm so sorry but you scared me!"

My shaken friend apologised.

But the taxi driver replied, "It's entirely my fault! You see, today is my first day driving a taxi....
for the previous twenty years, I drove a hearse!!"

Just been confirmed as the writer/director of the new Paddington 3 movie. I intend to go in a new direction and combine my love of Paddington Bear with films with epic battle scenes. So, 'Paddington the BraveHat!' should be in cinemas at Christmas 2023!

16. Meanwhile In Another Part Of This Book.....

INT. A BOOK PUBLISHER'S OFFICE.

GRAMS: PAPERBACK WRITER BY THE BEATLES

PUBLISHER: Yes, very interesting book. Very interesting book indeed, Mr Gotobed.

ROB: Oh thank you very much.

PUBLISHER: If I remember correctly we gave you a £950,000 advance, and after just six months, you produce this remarkable work of fiction.

ROB: Should be a bestseller, I think!

PUBLISHER: Well, it should be. You've lifted enough segments from other bestsellers.

ROB: Why, whatever do you mean?

PUBLISHER: Well? Take this excerpt. **(He reads from the book)** "Kravchenko was six when he killed his first agent. By the age of twenty, his reputation as an assassin was made. Kravchenko entered the hotel bedroom and crossed the room. His cold Russian finger trembling on the trigger. Olga felt her blood run cold. ...." Do I need to go on?

ROB: Well, that kind of thing happens everyday.

PUBLISHER: Not in a bloody cookery book it doesn't!!

ROB: Was that the recipe for Oeufs a la Crecy?

PUBLISHER: Yes, that was the recipe for Oeufs a la Crecy!

ROB: I got that recipe off Lee Child you know.

PUBLISHER: I know. I've just had his lawyers on the phone. Do you think perhaps you are insane?

ROB: No, not at all. ….Frogspawn!

PUBLISHER: Well, I've had another complaint from Clive Cussler, about your recipe for the 'Buttered prawns with potato and pea salad'.

ROB: Why?

PUBLISHER: Well, let me quote, from your book Mr Gotobed. "Plunge the prawns into boiling salted water. Then add two tablespoons of olive oil, whilst attempting to gun run in Guatemala. **(His voice starts to rise)** Then heat the mixture in a sultry pre-heated oven with a team of Mexican bandits who know no fear".

ROB: Yes, very delicious.

PUBLISHER: He's threatening to sue! Not only that but my wife tried the recipe and hasn't been seen for three weeks. Then this morning, I received a ransom demand together with this picture of a soufflé.

ROB: That's ludicrous!

PUBLISHER: Ah, at last we agree on something.

ROB: Certainly do. **......** I haven't put in a recipe for a soufflé.

PUBLISHER: Also yesterday**,** following your recipe for curried noodles, my mother-in-law was thrown out of Tesco's for shouting "You're only supposed to blow the bloody doors off!" when asked how many noodles she wanted. I wouldn't mind, but it's not even an Italian recipe!!

ROB: (In a Michael Caine voice) That's strange, The Italian Job's not supposed to be in season? Hmm?

PUBLISHER: Well, what about this little gem on page 82. "The Ford Anglia sailed high into the air, leaving Hogwarts and the quidditch game far, far below!" **(Pause)** It's Harry Potter isn't it?

ROB: No!

PUBLISHER: It's Harry Potter isn't it?

ROB: (More sincerely) No!

PUBLISHER: It's Harry bloody Potter isn't it?!?

ROB: (Shouting) Okay yes, but with crisp courgette tart!!

PUBLISHER: Maybe so, but it's still plagiarism. Now get out!

GRAMS: PAPERBACK WRITER BY THE BEATLES

"Hello this is your captain speaking. I am sorry to inform you that I have fallen out of the aeroplane lol. Mind you, I'm very impressed with the range on this Bluetooth headset!"

17. The Legend Of Ricky Slaughter!

It was early in the fourteenth century, about 7.30am in the morning actually, that the town of Cricklewood had fallen into a state of decline.

Since the death of the good Sheriff of Cricklewood, the town had fallen into the hands of his evil stepbrother from the North. **(F/X horses shrieking with fear).**

Ethelred the Trump, as he was known, was so evil that both The Wicked Witch of the West and the Child Catcher from Chitty Chitty Bang Bang came to him for lessons on how to be evil.

Immediately on his arrival he promptly awarded himself a humongous pay rise and increased the local taxes fifty fold. This made him extremely rich, while the inhabitants of Cricklewood got even poorer, in fact they became so poor that the local church mice set up a food bank for them.

However, help was at hand! A young man whom he had once sentenced to death for "looking at him in a funny way" was now, together with his merry band of outlaws, planning his downfall.

From their allotment on the edge of Strawberry Tump,

they would set off on raids to ambush vital supplies on the way to the Sheriff's castle.

They would then take their haul and share it among the locals, sometimes it was food, sometimes it was money, and sometimes, but only ever so occasionally, it was the Crown Jewels of England! Whatever is was, the people were glad to see the one they called, 'Ricky Slaughter!'

One member of his gang was Farty Partridge, whom Ricky met one day when he came upon him panting heavily, for which Farty apologised saying, "Sorry I'm out of breath but I've been breathing all day!" To this Ricky replied, "What is your village doing for an idiot while you're here?" Farty replied solemnly, "Nothing it's my day off!"

Another member of the notorious gang was Little John the Lollipop Man, who in an earlier escapade had locked lollipop sticks with Ricky on Ye Olde Zebra Crossing just in front of Cricklewood Castle.

The true love of Ricky's life was a young woman known as Maid Ceri-Anne, the daughter of a wealthy muck-spreading entrepreneur. He first met her some several summers past when she jumped out naked from behind a very high hedge, and after she robbed him of his Lincoln Green, he knew it was lust at first sight.

Incidentally, clothing manufactures who may be reading this, may be interested to know that in order to make Lincoln Green, they should first give him two tablespoons of castor oil.

Ricky and his gang constantly ambushed the Sheriff's men, until one day a sign pinned to a local farmer was brought to Ricky's attention. The sign read: 'Archery Competition to be held at Cricklewood Castle. A prize of 20 gold pieces to the winner.'

Ricky took that to mean 20 very, very small pieces of gold but he still decided to enter the competition under the pseudonym, Arnold Sidebottom. But first, he would have to get a new bow.
- Well, the high winds at the castle made such a mess of his hair!!

When Ricky and his gang arrived at the castle, there was some Morris dancing, but then he suddenly pulled a hamstring and that left only Arthur dancing.

When Maid Ceri-Anne arrived, Ricky asked her what she thought about his disguise? "I love the patch over the right eye", she replied. "But, I'm not so sure about the patch over your left eye?"

"Who said that?" said Ricky.

Then after several rather dull events, including pin the whip mark to the peasant's back, Ringing the Bull (don't ask?), Toad in the Hole (again don't ask?) and Pitch Penny (ask Penny), the Archery Competition began.

First to shoot was The Black Dove, who completely missed the target. But luckily for Ricky, Maid Ceri-Anne was there to pull the arrow out of his bottom.

Then after two other contestants had similarly hit Ricky in his bottom, it came to his turn.

Maid Ceri-Anne softly whispered "good luck" in Ricky's ear and with a steadfast arm and much precision, Ricky carefully took aim. Then after what appeared to be an eternity, but was in fact 5 or 6 Julian Calendar seconds, he pulled the string of his bow back as far as it would go and with an almighty 'twang' he sent his own personalised arrow shooting through the air.

It hit the target right in the bullseye which brought roars of cheers from both Maid Ceri-Anne and the onlookers, but not from the unfortunate bull, from which only came roars of pain.

Ricky received his prize of 20 exceedingly small gold pieces from the Sheriff himself. At this point in time, the

Sheriff did not recognise this particular outlaw's face, but in later exchanges the Sheriff was to become all too familiar with the face of Ricky Slaughter!

Ricky: You don't know who I am, do you?

Sheriff: No sir I do not. Do you know who I am?

Ricky: No, not sure, but your handlebar moustache seems to ring a bell!!

"Never put off until tomorrow what you can get a child to do today, simply by telling them you'll time them!"

18. How To Make Your Own Rob Gotobed Pregnancy Testing Kit!

You will need to steal:

1. A ruler – wooden or metal it makes no difference.

2. A piece of string bigger than your girlfriend's normal waist size. (If you do not have any string, spaghetti will do just as good.)

3. A paper and a pencil. Or a pen and a notebook. Or a cell phone and a finger.

You will then need to carefully carry out the following instructions:

1. Before sexual intercourse measure your girlfriend's midriff using the string/spaghetti and the ruler, wooden or metal.

2. Record the result on the piece of paper, or in your notebook, or on your phone and store somewhere safe.

3. Repeat the same procedure after sexual intercourse, and subtract the two figures.

Spoiler Alert!! The answer should be 0 (zero).

4. Continue the measurements daily, plotting the results on a graph: a consistent rise in waist size over a period of nine months tells you exactly what you need to know.

"The little voice inside your head that says nobody will ever love you? It's got to be getting that information from somewhere, right?"

My great-great-great grandmother was the only woman killed in the American Civil War battle at Gettysburg on July 2nd 1863. She wasn't in the battle, she was camping in the field next door and went over to complain about the noise!

19. Driving Down To Kraftwerk's Kling Klang Studio

8.05 am

Today I am taking a scenic drive down to Kraftwerk's Kling Klang studio in Germany. I am going there to do some recording for my new comedy album.

The sun is shining, the sky is blue and there are no clouds in the sky. It's my favourite part of the world and my favourite time of the year.

8.10 am

Everything is well with the world! I'm singing the song The Model by Kraftwerk and nothing's gonna stop me now!

8.12am

Just been pulled over by a German policeman. He wants to know why there are polar bear paw prints on the roof of my car? ......I genuinely have no idea!

I suggest he is mistaken and that they are not really polar bear paw prints but snowshoe prints made by some energetic skier who's used my roof as a short cut!

He explains to me that even though the paws of a polar bear act like snowshoes, "as the paws are wide and covered with fur to help the polar bear from slipping on ice and snow and that the thick black pads are covered with bumps to prevent slippage on ice", these are not snowshoe prints but 100% genuine polar bear paw prints!

Trust me to get pulled over by Germany's leading polar bear expert who happens to be a police patrol-man on his days off!!

So, I say to him, "Do you know how they catch polar bears? To which he replies "no!" So I say, "well you cut a hole in the ice and line it with peas! Then when the polar bear goes to take a pea, you sneak up behind him, and kick him in the ice-hole!"

8.25 am

Local German policeman does not appear to appreciate my British sense of humour!

He then explains that he's been following me for 16.09344 kilometres, I say why don't we just call it 10 miles, he repeats that he's been following me for 16.09344 kilometres!

He states that, unbeknown to me, he's been following me ever since I picked up an uninvited stowaway, aka Cocoa the world famous tap-dancing polar bear who had recently escaped from the Berlin Zoo and was making his way back home! Via it appears, the roof of my car!

I make a witty reply to this new information by saying, "Is it true that if you encounter a polar bear or a policeman who wants to talk about polar bears, that you should remain completely still and hope they lose interest?"

The local German policeman, it now appears, has NO sense of humour at all and demands to see my driving licence!

Unfortunately for me, two days prior to our meeting I had my latest course of Botox injections! Which means, that the expression on my face does not match the photo on my driver's licence and he wants to arrest me.

8.34 am

Thought for new tweet for Twitter: There's nothing wrong with aging, unless you're a cheese!

8.35 am

German Policeman tells me it is illegal to taxi around polar bears on the roofs of cars, especially between EU countries. He also wants to know if I voted for Brexit?

8.38am

I tell him I am not a taxi for polar bears, that I didn't vote for Brexit, and that I need to get home because I have to rehearse for next week's cameo in The Mentalist!

8.42 am

I tell him I'm playing "face down dead body in a living room." Where maid screams, wife calls lawyer, analyst, gynaecologist, Tibetan Guru, hairdresser, ….and then finally 911!

8.49 am

Policeman says The Mentalist is his favourite American TV series and will arrange for me to rehearse on floor of local German police station.

8.51 am

I don't think this is a very good idea, and try to remonstrate with the officer. But the police officer is having none of it and insists, complete with handcuffs, that I now go with him to rehearse at the local German police station.

9.34 am

We arrive at the local German police station, and I do some rehearsing. I lie on cold cell floor, get into "dead guy" character, but it is quite hard to do without a carpet!

10.35 am

Did not go well at local German police station. While rehearsing "face down dead body in a living room" (on cold cell floor) one of the two prison inmates with whom I am now sharing a cell with says, "how's the stand-up going, Rob?"

Worried about the impact this will have on next week's performance on The Mentalist...and any future Emmy hopes!?!?

12.58 am
Finally arrive at Kraftwerk's Kling Klang studio. What a relief!!

12.59 am
I will never forget that German Policeman's face though - it looked like a sad face that someone had drawn onto their scrotum!

"Heaven knows what girls see in my friend Neil? All he ever does is just sit at the bar licking his eyebrows with his tongue!"

20. Rob Gotobed's Christmas Message

My dearest readers, I wonder if, at this time of year, that I may ever so humbly beg as to have your momentary attention in order to discharge a by no means disobliging obligation which has over the years become an established tradition, within comedic circles, which is that of producing a traditional Christmas blog or message.

I may? Oh good. So here we go!

Britney was just twenty-one years old when she first met RAF Group Captain Rob Gotobed at a party in New York City.

There was something about him as soon as he entered the room. He looked very lost in his attire of long night shirt and night cap accompanied as he was by the Ghost of Christmas Present!

So I made my excuses to the gentleman I was talking to, I think I said something like "I need to go for a poo!" and then I went over and introduced myself to this strange Ebenezer Scrooge tribute band.

"Hi!" I said, "I'm Britney, I'm a digital analyst and marketing advisor" and held out my hand.

I will never forget the glazed expression that appeared on Rob Gotobed's face when he said, "Absolutely amazing that, Ghost of Christmas Present, I know these are only ghostly visions of the present and that no one can actually see or hear me, but by golly, I would swear that this young lady can actually see me!"

And I will never forget The Ghost of Christmas Present's reply, "She can you Wazzock! I keep telling you, you're getting confused with Charles Dickens Christmas Carol, we've moved on a bit since 1843! Mind you, saying that, due to all the cutbacks in the spiritual world, in order to save on ectoplasm we now have to cut back on our ghostly apparitions. So, instead of you being invisible when we do this part, we actually just take you for a walk around the area where you actually live on Christmas Eve. But we still seem to get the desired effect!

Mind you, the Ghosts of Christmas Past and Future haven't had to endure the cutbacks we have, in fact their budgets have increased! Apparently, it's more expensive these days to conjure up ghostly images of the past and future".

Rob then said, "what a fine woman indeed this Britney is, would you not agree Ghost of Christmas Present?" "She certainly is, nice fine figure, ample, pouting breasts and such firm thighs that you could use them to crack open your walnuts!" replied the Ghost of Christmas Present.

"I can hear you both!" I replied.

"Ooh sorry Britney, I keep forgetting that! I'm old school you see!" replied the Ghost.

But then, at that very instant, the main doors to the hall flew open and who should be standing there but Donald Trump himself!

But it was not the Donald Trump of old! No more the black pantaloons, strutting codpiece and dark, foreboding expressions of hate.

Instead, there before them stood the merriest of old gentlemen, wearing a ruby red waistcoat bordered with white fur. The waistcoat hung so loosely on his bare breasted chest that it could barely conceal the white hairs of his aged torso. On his face was the broadest, warmest smile that anyone living had ever seen, and in his arms were a veritable cornucopia of gifts.

"Merry Christmas, one and all! May I come in and get to know you all better?" said Donald in a robustious voice.

"For look upon me, I am born again!" He retorted!

"God bless us everyone!" remarked Rob in a very theatrical and camp manner.

"Hang on, we're all getting out of sync here!" said the Ghost of Christmas Present.

"Is this more of your handy work?" I enquired of the Ghost.

"Yes!" replied the Ghost of Christmas Present, "I had Donald a couple of hours ago, the Ghost of Christmas Yet To Come must have just finished with him!"

"Wow! What a transformation?" I exclaimed!

"Yes, quite!" said the Ghost.

"God bless us everyone!" remarked Rob in a very

theatrical and camp manner.

"Shut up Rob!" said I and the Ghost together.

At that very moment Donald approached Rob from across the long ballroom floor. He ran as he crossed the room with his arms outstretched in front of him.

"Ah, my dear friend Rob", chuckled Donald as he fully embraced him and kissed him on both cheeks.

"I've seen the error of my ways! Tomorrow I want you to start to work for me, but at double the salary Jimmy Fallon and Seth Myers are paying you. And, I want you to become a fully fledged partner in the firm of Trump & Gotobed! What do you say old buddy, old friend? Or should I say Bro?" and then Donald attempted to do a cool rapper's hand gesture for Rob to slam his fist into.

There followed a momentary silence that seemed to last an eternity, and then Rob grabbed the crutch that stood idle next to the chair of Tiny Rudy Giuliani and smashed it into the head of Donald Trump, "I am not bloody Bob Scratchit! Get that into your thick head. And you are not

Scrooge, you're a pathetic old man that nobody will ever like, no matter how nice you are! Understand?"

But Donald could not understand, and nothing would ever go into his head again. He was dead! Quite, quite dead!

There was no doubt whatsoever about that, Old Trump was dead as a door nail, although come to think of it, there is nothing particularly dead about a door nail. But there is no doubt that Trump was dead. This must be distinctly understood, or nothing wonderful can come of this story I have related!

And so, as Rob Gotobed observed, "God Bless Us Every One!"

"I ate a 'Chef Special' for lunch today and I'm not even a chef! Come and get me Food Police - I have a huge start and you'll never find me!"

"I still can't really tell at a McDonald's drive-thru if their employee is reaching out for my payment, or just for me to kiss their hand!"

21. Ugh The Elder Leads An Uprising Against The Romans

By the year 60BC, England was made up of many genial and hospitable tribes, each with their own chef – sorry, I think that should read chief.

In Cricklewood, the Cricklewood Boys as they were affectionately known were under the rule of Ugh the Elder, who ran the local fruit and Uber franchise.

Ugh got his name because ever since his childhood people had pointed at him and said, "Ugh!"

When Ugh's diary was recently uncovered in the local Cricklewood quarry, etched in the stone of a sheer cliff, it proved to be a unique discovery of a most remarkable contemporary document.

Each page a foot high telling in detail the story of a week in Ugh's life. Page one being at the bottom of the cliff, page two above that and so on. Ugh is believed to have died falling from the unfinished page six hundred and thirty two.

Ugh's chronicle tells us of how the peaceful world of England was soon to be shattered, for in Rome greedy eyes were looking north.

In 55BC (Ugh places it at 11.30am on August the 5th) Julius Caesar took his legions for a well deserved holiday to sun drenched England. Well, they had been working hard and he had promised them one! It was an event which was to have a drastic effect on the old English way of life.

Caesar arrived with 12,000 men (you know, what Cricklewood Football Club used to get on a Saturday back in the sixties), but although they only spent about two weeks camped on Cricklewood beach, they vowed that they would return one day, complete with woolly underwear.

Such threats held no fear for the men of Cricklewood, even though the Romans were well known throughout Europe for enjoying holidays consisting of fighting, pillage, debauchery and grapes. Not to mention their other very annoying habit of putting their towels on swimming pool sun loungers and beach huts.

And so in the fateful summer of AD 43, the fierce and mighty Roman Expeditionary Force stormed the beach at Cricklewood.

Previous to this attack the Romans had conquered the whole of the South of England in just over a fortnight. But because the Cricklewood Boys were "superior warriors" compared to the Southern 'Nancy' boys", it took the Romans a lot longer to conquer the Cricklewood beach and municipal swimming pool.

However, this, they eventually achieved by building a legionary fortress on the hill overlooking Cricklewood.

The fortress was elegantly designed and very colourful – and so it should be, since the Romans stole all the colourful beach huts along Cricklewood promenade to build it. In fact it was so colourful even Walt Disney would have been impressed.

The Romans built their fortress right next door to where Mrs Washington used to teach in Castle Street. (It's a small world isn't it?) They had also planned to build Caesar's Palace here, but could not get planning permission, so they built it in Las Vegas instead.

At first Ugh and the Cricklewood Boys got on well with the Romans, as the majority of them were employed on their Youth Opportunity Progamme building their roads and houses. That was until the Romans who spoke Latin decided to change the name of Cricklewood to 'Matulae Hominum', which was fine, till someone pointed out to

Ugh that in English it translated to 'Men's Urinals!'

Well that was it! ….WAR!!

So, Ugh and his men invited The Romans to a rumble just outside the old town gates on the site where the Nooky Nooky massage parlour is today. Thinking they had been invited to a ramble (bad translation by their interpreter) the Romans readily agreed and dressed suitably for the occasion, with sandals and sunglasses, and armed with a selection of soft grapes and wines.

This was a big mistake and Ugh and his men charged the Romans as soon as they appeared.

The battle lasted for forty days and forty nights (in those days things had a habit of dragging on), but at the final whistle neither side had won a decisive victory.

Which is really strange because you'd think that during those forty days and forty nights that at least one bright spark amongst the Romans would have gone and got their weapons and shields, but oh no, they just carried on squirting suntan lotion at Ugh's men and kicking sand in their faces.

A replay was organised for the same time next year and they all went home for some tea and Cannolis.

Thus was the Roman occupation of my home town of Cricklewood, which lasted until sometime around AD 383 when Maximum 'Headroom' Magnus called upon all his soldiers in England to catch the last chariot home.

And so that was that, except for the fact that some of you may be asking yourselves "where does the name 'Roman' originate from?" Well, apparently, it derives from the first invasion of England, when in a hurry to get there, the Legionnaire in charge of the oarsmen would cry out, "Row man row!" And so they became known as Romans.

Anyway, that's what my great-grandfather told me when I was a child.

> ***"Let's see what happens if we all stop at the next iPhone!"***

22. Human Spontaneous Combustion

'Human Spontaneous Combustion', is it an embarrassing problem? "Not anymore", says top British Scientist Rob Gotobed.

"Anyone can suffer from spontaneous combustion, and believe me, it can be very embarrassing! Whether it be standing at a urinal in a restroom, during sexual intercourse, or entertaining at a kids party as Uncle Bonzo, the exploding balloon clown, and **'WHOOSH! BOOM! SPLAT!!!'** you explode into a fireball of towering flames.

In the past people presumed that Human Spontaneous Combustion (HSC) was caused as a side-effect of erectile dysfunction. But this is simply not true, and believe me when I say, I should know!

So what can you do to reduce the risks of HSC? Well, why not try my NEW-and-improved 'Rob Gotobed fire retardant boxer shorts!'

They are fairly comfortable, they don't smell (well, not much) and they keep fire down to manageable proportions. They have an inbuilt fart-activated sprinkler system, a snug PBI coating and an emergency escape hatch. - "Hello and help!"

Yes, my all new, anti-spontaneous combustion underpants are only available from the new online Rob

Gotobed Novelty Gift Shop. ......And at only $9.99 plus tax, they are a real bargain!

But don't take my word for it – I have hundreds, well two actually, satisfied potential victims."

"Hi, I've been wearing Rob Gotobed's fire retardant boxer shorts for eighteen years, and I have not exploded once!" (Daniel Craig, aka James Bond).

"I've been wearing the same pair of Rob Gotobed's fire retardant boxer shorts for ten years now, but I am thinking of buying a second pair!" (Donald Trump, The White House USA)

Disclaimer: Please be warned, Rob Gotobed's Fire Retardant Boxer Shorts® do have a tendency to catch fire if exposed to oxygen at temperatures in excess of 5 degrees Celsius.

Also, this week sees the long awaited release of 'The Rob Gotobed Book on Ancient Pyramidism', it is priced $169 plus tax, or FREE with all good packets of 'Gotobed's Delicious Cocoa Nuggets!'

In the book Prof. Rob Gotobed answers the question: What is it about the ancient pyramid shape that has such life-preserving qualities?

For example: A pineapple placed under a pyramid will stay fresh for longer than a pineapple kept under a hat.

To prove my theory, I, Prof. Rob Gotobed, have spent six months living under a large glass pyramid, and now, amazingly enough, I too look like a pineapple!!"

"Did you know, that you can get the same effect of hearing the ocean from a seashell just by putting your ear right up against someone's bellybutton and listening closely!"

Don't you think The Rolling Stones are being very optimistic when they still sing 'Time Is On My Side'!!

23. MacKing's Burger Drive-Thru Sex Scam! PLEASE BE WARNED!!

My girlfriend has recently become a victim of a clever scam which is spreading across the UK.

The scam happens while you are sitting in your car at your local 'MacKing's Burger Drive Thru' waiting for your burger and fries.

Here's how the scam works: Two extremely good-looking 22-24 year-old males will come over to your girlfriend's car as she is waiting for her burger and fries at the Drive-Thru. After they have removed their shirts to reveal, in my girlfriend's words, "their very firm, golden tanned six-packs, wide shoulders and strong and warm arms", they will both start to clean her windscreen. When she thanks them and offers them a tip, they will both say 'no' and instead ask her for a lift to a specific destination, in my girlfriend's case it was to the local Primark store.

When your girlfriend agrees to give them a lift, the two males will both get into the back seat of the car. Then on the way, they will start undressing until both are completely NAKED!!

Then, when your girlfriend pulls over to get a selfie, one of them climbs over into the front seat and starts crawling all over her lap, kissing her, touching her intimately, and thrusting himself against her, while the other one steals her handbag.

My girlfriend has had her handbag stolen on May 4th, 9th,10th, twice on the 15th, 17th, 20th, 24th and 25th!

On June 26th, 27th, 28th, 29th, and twice this morning!

So please, PLEASE warn all the women you know to be on the lookout for this scam.

According to my girlfriend these guys seem to be particularly active just before lunch and at about 4:30pm in the afternoon.

She also informs me that Primark have cheap handbags on sale for £14.99 each. Although their handbags at £15.75 look a lot more expensive! – But I don't understand why that's relevant?!?!?

Please don't be naive enough to think that it couldn't happen to you or your girlfriend!!!

"What exactly was going on in my life when I decided to give YogurBerry my email address?"

24. Rob Gotobed Astrologer Extraordinaire!

Welcome to another look at 'The Love Stars' with me Mystic Rob Gotobed, the all-seeing, the all-knowing, the all-dancing astrologer extraordinaire!

So, without more to do, let's see what the 'Love Stars' have in store for YOU over the coming weeks.

There is much upheaval among the stars this month, as Jupiter moves into the house of Aries, Aries goes to stay in Gemini's house for the weekend, and Saturn moves into the house of Taurus for a nominal rent while the builders damp-proof her rings!!

If today is your birthday?
A special event could happen sometime during the day. You will be receiving mail from friends and relatives. There is a strong possibility of cake, and you may be feeling a little bit older. You will also meet a stranger though he may not talk to you, and please, please, try not to go near any escaped Bengal tigers!!

AQUARIUS
Another peaceful and tranquil month for Aquarians, who by their very nature are gentle, non-violent people. Romance, adventure and wealth all await you.

PISCES
You will be feeling moody and restless. The moon in the sky probably means it is night, while the sun in your hair

probably means you are starring in a shampoo advert. A good month for getting some of your Aquarian friends to go and pickup the shopping for you.

ARIES
You will do well to remember that the clothes you wear to the office will not be suitable for the swimming pool. Especially, if you intend to dive off the diving board! I think you know what I'm trying to say here!

Remember Aries, that hope can always be found in the bottom of a Chinese curry.

TAURUS
You will be transported back to 1984 in a Delorean car where, frustratingly, no one will believe you when you say that in the future people will carry telephones in their pockets and have televisions the size of Mount Rushmore!

You will then be committed to a psychiatric hospital when you explain that Donald Trump is The President of The United States of America and that Boris Johnson is the Prime Minister of Great Britain. You will never ever be released from the insane asylum. Sorry!!

GEMINI
A good period for attending to money-matters. All of your wishes can come true if you're willing to briefly take on a life of crime. So, why not form a gang and go and rob a few banks. Remember it is always good to have a

few Aquarians in the gang just in case you need one or two fall guys.

CANCER
You are generally very earthy, which may mean that you don't shower as often as most people. That is something you may wish to address this month if love is to come your way. Probably be best to partner up with an Aquarian, who by design have no sense of smell.

LEO
Wherever Leos go they should expect comedy and laughter to ensue. This would be great if you were the ones trying to be funny, but unfortunately, everyone is laughing at you, not with you!

People born under Leo are deeply confused by the idea of sex. They also have a strong compulsion to wear long floaty 'hippy' dresses, together with enormous amounts of makeup and unusual jewellery made from llama droppings.

Find a best friend who is an Aquarian, then renegotiate deadlines if need be.

VIRGO
Virgos love to be the centre of attention. They love nothing more than to walk around the house in the middle of the night, 'starkers', with the lights out and to hell with the consequences and injuries.

A flirtation in the workplace with a Scorpio may help to lift your spirits, but be warned, this does not include the spirits in your mini bar!

This flirtation may also bring with it other dangers, because even if you are both free, this kind of liaison isn't advisable, as dating a Scorpio could be playing with fire. This is due to the fact that Scorpions, by their very nature, are evil to the bone and are the devil in human form. (Please see Scorpio below for details)

LIBRA
Today I see Pluto rising which is a good sign, but because Mickey Mouse and Goofy are not getting up till much later in the afternoon that could be a sign of imminent danger! So you would do well to beware any ducks wearing a sailor shirt and cap.

Star formations are very important in astrology, for example The Big Dipper, The Plough and The Bear but you need to be aware this month, as these are also the names of the three pubs in Cricklewood you will get thrown out of for being drunk and disorderly.

Also, this would be a good month to get yourself a lucky charm. I myself have a rabbit's foot, although it did start off as an ingrowing toenail.

But remember, Librans are among the most civilized of the zodiacal characters and are often good looking, short, ugly and have no fashion sense. A happy phase, but take care not to tire yourself out.

Don't scam too many Aquarians!

SCORPIO
People born under Scorpio are nothing more than human scorpions.

They are easily recognisable because they have eight legs, two of which are a giant pair of grasping pedipalps and a narrow segmented ass often carried in a characteristic forward curve over their back, ending with an evil and venomous stinger. - Well, at least my ex-wife does!

They like nothing more than smashing the male of the species with their bare hands and taunting him about the size of his manhood.

They usually make good business women because they have a lack of both morals and ethics and they would sooner sustain crippling injuries than do anything the easy way. Again, I may be confusing ex-wives here with scorpions.

Anyway, sometimes you feel there just aren't enough hours in the day. You must learn to delegate.

Also, an ex-loved one may be being picky and critical, they may not be going about it in the most helpful way, but "hey!" why not give them an opening!

SAGITTARIUS
Sagittarians are generally ambidextrous, which means that they can pick both sides of their nose at the same time, while holding a cup of coffee in one hand and fiddling a violin with the other.

Sagittarians tend to be nothing more than paranoid Aquarians. However, avoid becoming self-critical and try not to overthink matters. Arrange for yourself and a few friends to go and laugh at some Aquarians.

CAPRICORN
A time for prudence! If my birthday was on the cusp with Aquarians I would keep very, very quiet about it!!

If you would like to hear more about how 'Comet Trump' will give you the power to get the future you've dreamed of? Then call Mystic Rob Gotobed's 01 0800-AstroVague, the number one premium phone service for astrological forecasts of a vague, one-size-fits-all nature.

Calls from both landlines and cellphones cost almost $250 per minute.

And finally, there will be some breaking news from the BBC later today, when it is announced that due to new European regulations, all apples will be required to state clearly the number of pips they contain.

Be seeing you!!

"Whenever I use my car to get somewhere quickly and comfortably, I can't help but wonder why people in the past were so addicted to their wagons?"

25. Taylor Swift In Rob Gotobed Stalking Shock!

The tabloids are afire this week with the stunning news that Taylor Swift, the "feisty" twosome who was plucked from obscurity and transformed into one of America's most successful double acts (the biggest since Simon & Garfunkel, Hall and Oates and of course, Trump and Pence) has been accused of "allegedly" stalking Rob Gotobed of Rob Gotobed fame.

The stunning allegations, which have stunned the entertainment world, were made after what appears to be a string of "mysterious circumstances" surrounding Mr. Gotobed, known around the world for his huge talent, huge stardom and of course his Hugh Jackman!

"I have been in hiding for the last six months" Mr. Gotobed told me from his concrete bunker at a secret location at 23 Appledumpling Street, Cricklewood. "It has been a nightmare. Just because I am in the public eye, it doesn't mean my life is up for any old Tom, Dick or Deborah Harry to hound my every move."

The whole sorry tale started in September 2019, when Mr. Gotobed returned home to find his garbage had been knocked over in a seemingly random attack by Taylor Swift.

"That is typical of Taylor," he confided. "She is well known for being a bit of a loose cannon when it comes to the law, and doesn't even care what the neighbours say. She has absolutely no regard. I am stunned."

Mr. Gotobed claims the attacks have become more intensified since his rendition of 'Shake It Off' on Japanese Television. He says his windows have been egged on a regular basis, and his suspicions immediately fell upon the well-known urban elf, Taylor Swift.

"I know Taylor is not probably known for this kind of mindless vandalism but she is easily egged on – and so is my house!".

Mr. Gotobed, resplendent in matching red feather boa and Y-fronts, just wishes to be left alone by the terrible teenybopper.

"I blame Emma Watson. She is the brains of the operation and I just know whenever I see one of her intimidating films that she is thinking of all kinds of wicked, wicked things to do to me."

When questioned further about Emma Watson, Mr. Gotobed shuddered and told us of waking up one morning and being stunned to find Clarins Joli Rouge lipstick daubed on his front door. This, he tells us, is her calling card.

Both Taylor Swift and Emma Watson's management have stunningly refused to comment on the accusations, and Mr. Gotobed is living in fear for his life.

A sobbing Mr Gotobed also told us that he hates any kind of publicity! He then asked us to tell all our friends on social media, and any journalists we may know, about what has happened to him to avoid it happening to someone else.

BREAKING NEWS: **Taylor Swift and Emma Watson are actually doing community service in Cricklewood, after a complaint was received about them kicking a football against a pensioner's bungalow in the early hours.

Both still refuse to apologise to Mr. Gotobed, and if asked by anyone will actually deny all knowledge of their reign of terror.

Report By *Izzy Ferrari* 14th April 2020

"Why are there still TV adverts for bread? Who still doesn't know about bread?"

26. Rob Gotobed: Another 22 Things You Never Knew!

1. Rob Gotobed is one of the few people who believe Roger Rabbit was guilty.

2. American scientists are working on a robot version of Rob Gotobed to go and entertain the unmanned drones in Afghanistan.

3. Rob believes that everything he draws with his magic crayon comes to life.

4. In 1892, Rob Gotobed was cryogenically frozen for 100 years in his great-grandfather's fridge.

5. Rob frequently participates in staring contests with the sun, and always wins!!

6. Rob has never sneezed and his farts smell of elderberries.

7. Rob once ruptured a disc playing Rock Band: Roadie Edition.

8. Rob is banned from the Deadwood branch of Dunkin' Donuts.

9. Rob says, "The hardest thing about being the REAL JAMES BOND is not telling the world"

10. It took Rob Gotobed 2 minutes and 28 seconds to solve The Da Vinci Code.

11. The crack in Rob Gotobed's bottom is the exact same shape as the lightening mark on Harry Potter's forehead.

12. After every comedy performance, his favourite treat is to lick his knees clean with his tongue.

13. He once ate a very small car.

14. In 2010, Rob Gotobed claimed to have discovered the clitoris and invented the wheel.

15. In 2011, he claimed he had found the Holy Grail - which he now keeps safe in his girlfriend's handbag.

16. In 2012, he got into a bar fight with Megatron, Optimus Prime, and The Predator ....And Won!!

17. Rob has two sets of testicles, neither of which are his own and his urine is bottled by a major soft drinks company.

18. According to reliable sources, Rob Gotobed's naked body looks like the discount rack in an Old Navy store.

19. Rob Gotobed has a pet dolphin called Russell which he keeps in a hutch he built himself.

20. According to his Management, Rob Gotobed will completely shed his skin up to five times during his comedy shows.

21. Every Thursday evening Rob likes to go to his local McDonald's just for the free mustard sachets.

22. Rob Gotobed claims to be the only person on Earth who knows the real identity of Superman.

NB. All facts were correct at time of going to press.

"I'd love to help you mate, but I got my own problems," said I, from inside a red Royal Mail post box.

27. Rob Gotobed's Reversible Toilet Paper!

Hi! My name is Rob Gotobed, and I run The Rob Gotobed Novelty Poop Shop!

Today's special offer....**Rob Gotobed's Reversible Toilet Paper!**

Yes, it's even better than recyclable toilet paper!

Yes, with my all-new, thicker, extra absorbent Gotobed toilet paper, you can now use both sides and then stick it on the washing line to dry, and then use it again!!

Each roll comes with a lifetime guarantee and is only $9.99 plus tax from The Rob Gotobed Novelty Poop Shop!

How does it work? I don't know, but believe me when I say, it does!!

**Please note: The Rob Gotobed Combined Toilet Brush & Nasal Comb Gift Set has had to be withdrawn for safety reasons!!

"Can't believe my two dogs just ran into 'Petsmart' and left me locked in the car with the windows rolled up!"

28. Rob Gotobed And Tony Knight's Almost Legendary Interview

Rob Gotobed and **Tony Knight** have spent so much time living in the USA, doing things such as making videos for the likes of Funny Or Die, you'd be mistaken for thinking they're American. In fact, Rob is originally from Cricklewood and Tony from Wimbledon in the United Kingdom.

After two years touring the USA, Rob and Tony are coming back to the UK to perform at The Leicester Square Theatre, in London's West End later this month.

Here they answer some of our random questions...

Hi guys. How are you?

ROB: Great. This morning I turned my 'Welcome' door mat around and went outside for the first time in six years.

TONY: I just had a cup of coffee that gave me just about enough energy to get up and find another cup of coffee.

ROB: Yeah, I can vouch for that. He drank so much caffeine this morning that his phone is charging simply by him holding it in his hand.

Where are you currently living?

TONY: We've rented a flat in Earl's Court.

ROB: It's great. We live right opposite a 24-hour supermarket. Which is great for all those times when you wake up at 3am and think "These curtains have GOT to go!"

How do you find British Police?

TONY: Brilliant. Anytime I've been in trouble with a police officer, I've usually eased the tension by just telling them to relax or to take a chill pill.

ROB: I always feel safer when I see traffic cops wearing those little white gloves, as I know if needed, they can direct me or make me a quality sandwich.

Were you interested in the recent General Election?

ROB: I just find it ridiculous that it's 2015 and Britain STILL hasn't elected a Prime Minister that has a shaved head with a really long, braided pony tail.

TONY: So how does this voting thing work again? Do we just unfollow the candidate we don't like?

Um… maybe Tony! How do you get on with modern technology?

TONY: I told a mate that my phone always autocorrects 'hahaha' to 'iguana'. The trouble is I've been trying to warn him about a killer iguana since last Friday and he thinks he's being hilarious.

ROB: My mum has an app that sends drone strikes.

Do either of you use social media?

ROB: Of course. In fact I just read a Facebook post describing something as "sir-real" and now I have a new favourite thing.

TONY: Twitter and Instagram fall out of a bar laughing about how good life is. They hear a voice begging for change; when they look down they see it's MySpace. Twitter and Instagram quickly sober up and hail a taxi.

ROB: My mother has more followers on Twitter than me.

Do you like watching cookery programmes like The Great British Bake Off?

TONY: Are you joking? We love them.

ROB: I wasn't alive when ravioli was invented, but I can only imagine the SHOCKWAVES it sent throughout the pasta-making community.

Do you believe in UFOs and aliens?

TONY: I believe we have already made contact with the aliens and they're way cooler than us. For example, they can skateboard forever without falling down.

ROB: Not sure, but if aliens do ever invade our planet the first question they'll have is 'Why is that tiger that loves cereals wearing a scarf?'

What about conspiracy theories... any you believe in?

TONY: Of course! I mean everybody knows that the real point of the Apollo space missions was to assassinate the first chimp in space who refused to return to Earth and declared himself Moon King.

ROB: I've never caught a bouquet at a wedding but I've been hit twice with a bag of rubbish from a moving car.

TONY: What the hell does that mean?

ROB: They know! ......They know!!

Do you find girls are more likely to make the first move since you've become known as The Fab Two?

TONY: Oh without a doubt. I was in a taxi with a young actress, only last week, whose name I will not divulge, and when we got to our destination the taxi driver said "that will be £15.80"... and this actress flashed him the map of Tasmania!

ROB: For those of your readers who are not too clever on geography. Tasmania is a triangular shaped island a bit on the bushy side...

TONY: Anyway to cut a long story short the taxi driver said, "Haven't you got anything smaller?"

What advice do you have for people going on a first date?

TONY: Well, a great idea for a first date is to eat a handful of caterpillars the day before. Then drink lots of Coca Cola and then right in the middle of the date - burp out a flock of beautiful butterflies. Never ceases to impress the girls.

ROB: Also, don't respond to texts right away or you might look desperate.

TONY: Yeah that's right, always wait a few years and then reply "not much, you?" Keep it casual.

ROB: I joined a Dating Agency once. They matched me with a Jane Austen novel and a bottle of Tequila.

Have either of you ever come up with a totally unique idea?

TONY: Yes, an edible vegan cookbook.

ROB: A t-shirt that reads "I DIDN'T POOP IN THERE, SOMEONE ELSE DID BUT IT WASN'T ME" to wear when exiting coffee shop toilets.

What's your favourite movie?

TONY: TOY STORY obviously, and the best thing about TOY STORY is that if they ever decide to make an 'adult' version they can keep the same theme song. (YOU'VE GOT A FRIEND IN ME!)

ROB: Do I have to shave? No? Cool. Do I have to talk? No? Great! Can I smash stuff up? Yeah? Awesome!! Count me in.

TONY: Who's that supposed to be?

ROB: Jason Statham signing a movie contract.

Earliest childhood memory?

ROB: Watching seagulls circle overhead with tears in my eyes, because it was impossible to tell which one had stolen my onion ring.

TONY: Threatening to hold my breath until I got the sweets I wanted. Then passing out on the pavement and coming around to see my mum standing over me saying, "I don't negotiate with terrorists".

Any other childhood memories?

TONY: That a simple joy of youth is telling another child you've caught a squirrel in a box trap, then dropping a cage on him when he goes to check.

Tell us a bit about your school days...

ROB: I was voted 'Most Paranoid' by my classmates. Although they never did admit it.

What sex education did either of you get at school?

TONY: None at all really. I remember once Mr Williams our headmaster requested all the boys to go to the main hall one afternoon after lunch. Then, when we had all gathered he addressed us, "Are we all here? Right shut the doors. Are they all shut? Yes, good. Very well. Now look here, if you touch it, it will fall off! Right, return to your classes". And that was it. I left equipped for life!

ROB: Have you noticed that all those in favour of birth control are already born?

Most luxurious thing you've experienced?

TONY: I once visited a restroom in New York that was so refined that as you entered a sushi chef sliced individual sheets of toilet paper from cedar logs.

ROB: I once got to ride on a diamond encrusted jet ski. By the way, did you know, if your jet ski catches on fire in a fjord the Norwegian Navy just raise their swords and drink a toast to you.

TONY: Yamaha is a weird company. You can stroll into one of their stores and ride out on a jet ski playing a keyboard. Very strange.

Rob, where did you get that hair style?

ROB: Giovanni's in the high street. They like to do things a little differently there.

TONY: That's right, when it's your turn you take a seat on a mechanical bull and they turn on the scissor fan.

ROB: I once saw Richard Branson walking in there holding up a picture of Iron Maiden's Eddie.

What is your most treasured item?

TONY: Well, Rob's would have to be that old chair he takes with him everywhere.

ROB: Listen mate, that broken recliner and I go way back...

What previous jobs have you had?

ROB: I use to work at Pizza Hut but I got fired because I kept saying "pasta la vista, baby" to people... Do you think I should include that on my resume?

What music are you into?

TONY: The Beatles obviously. Did you know that if you play The Beatles' SGT PEPPER'S album backwards it contains a really good Nut Roast recipe?

ROB: The music of Justin Bieber really speaks to me, because I am a hat.

Tell us a secret you've never told anybody else?

ROB: Every night my socks sneak out of my laundry basket, steal buttons from my clothes and go off to become Muppets.

TONY: One day man will swim to the moon.

Have you become friendly with any celebrities?

ROB: Russell Crowe **i**s in the pizza-making class I signed up for at Cricklewood Leisure Centre. It's true and, do you know what, he yells at the instructor almost every week.

TONY: Well, I can't name names but I can tell you one thing for sure. And that's Tom Cruise isn't even the star of his own home movies.

Did your parents ever give you good advice?

TONY: Yes, my mother once gave me a great bit of advice. She said, "Tony, you're not a real dinosaur and stop eating all those sweets!"

ROB: No! In fact kids, never listen to your parents... mine said I could never be a ninja turtle, but there I was last night in a sewer eating pizza with three other drunk dudes...

Nice. To end on, do you have a piece of really good advice for anyone reading this interview?

ROB: Leaving three Mexican sour gherkins on someone's doorstep in the middle of the night is a fairly inexpensive way to occupy a portion of their mind forever.

TONY: Go to your local card shop and hang out near the "I'm Sorry" greeting cards. Wait till someone comes over. Break wind. Hand them a card and walk away.

NOT JUST ROB GOTOBED BUT ALSO TONY KNIGHT' WILL BE ON AT THE LEICESTER SQUARE THEATRE ON SATURDAY 23RD MAY 2015.

"If I was a spy – which I'm NOT! If I was ever captured, all they'd have to do to get me to talk would be to put my shoes on the wrong feet!"

29. Captain Horatio Whiplash And His Ship The HMS Hesitant

Captain Horatio Whiplash, the famous 18th century adventurer was born in Cricklewood in the year 1670. Ever since he was a young lad he had dreamed of discovering new lands. So when he ran away from home at the age of 38, it wasn't long before he obtained a position on board his first ship.

The ship he joined was called HMS Love-A-Duck and it was whilst on board her that young Horatio first showed his propensity! .....He then had to clean all the poop up off the poop deck as a punishment for flashing his propensity around!!

It was whilst on board HMS Love-A-Duck that he began to study navigation, which turned out to be a really good idea, since up until this point nobody on board the ship ever had the slightest idea where the ship was located.

In those days the chief method of getting sailors for the Royal Navy was by means of what was called 'press gangs' whereby a bunch of journalists were allowed by law to go about the streets seizing men.

These press ganged sailors were either criminals or drunks, who all had one thing in common, they all wanted to leave the Royal Navy as soon as they could. In fact, during Captain Horatio Whiplash's famous last voyage, fifteen of the crew had jumped overboard before the ship had even left Plymouth harbour.

This led the Captain to write in his Ship's Log, Stardate 4385.3, that fatal Saturday night; "If we lose anymore of the crew at the present rate, I'll have to steer the ship my 'bloody' myself!"

Captain Horatio's ship for that fateful expedition was HMS Hesitant, a sister ship of the larger HMS Capsized and HMS Submerged. Originally he had intended to call his ship HMS Titanic but that idea sank.

The goal of his last journey was to find and bring back a Gorgon's head. This was the price the Captain had to pay for being the most successful sea captain in His Majesty's Royal Navy.

Throughout Cricklewood and England Captain Horatio Whiplash was a national hero, but recently he had upset a lot of the Admiralty with his views on "fake" news and his repeated threats to construct a large border wall around France, claiming that if he was elected 'Pope', he would "build the wall and make Mexico pay for it!"

Therefore the only way the King of England and the Admiralty could restore faith in themselves, was to discredit the nation's hero.

There were in fact three Gorgons. Once they had been beautiful women, but they had boasted about their beauty and so, legend has it, the gods punished their vanity by turning them into hideous monsters. A bit like what happened recently to the British Prime Minister Theresa May.

The task looked hopeless, but one night Horatio was visited by a God-like figure, which presented him with some useful gifts for his hazardous journey. 'H' put it down to the cheese and pickles he had eaten earlier that evening, but when the airy spirit, who resembled 'Jim Carrey', shouted **"Well a**lrighty then!" and dropped a metal sickle and shield into his lap, he soon sat up and began to take notice.

These he was given together with a pair of winged sandals, which really impressed his fellow men, since he could now fly up to the crow's nest without having to climb the ropes and risk being blown overboard.

Eventually, it is said, that he found the Gorgon's (it was next to the tonic all the time – Gordon's Gin get it?!?!) asleep among some rocks. Then by using his shield as a mirror, he crept forward and with one swift blow of his sword gave the Gorgon a cute centre parting to be proud of! But ungrateful as ever, this Gorgon was even more furious with her new hairstyle, so Horatio had to cut of her head and placed it in a bag-for-life!

He handed this bag to his second in command with instructions to take it back to the Admiralty in England with the message: "Here's something to get really stoned on!"

Since Horatio was now 95, he would not be returning to England with the rest of his crew but would remain in this strange new land they had discovered in 1765.

The land they had discovered was blessed with an overwhelming abundance of flora and fauna and the crew of HMS Hesitant had become preoccupied with giving names to every conceivable plant and animal they discovered.

Indeed as Captain Horatio Whiplash wrote in his Ship's Log, Stardate 4392.6, "a fist fight broke out today between two midshipmen, James Emu and Henry Cassowary, about who saw a large flightless bird first and who, therefore should have it named after him. Similarly, I had to step in between Messrs Alfred Eucalyptus and Ebenezer Platypus about a tree and an odd egg-laying amphibian we came across. The only way I could dissolve the dispute was also to agree to name our first encampment in this strange land after Ebenezer."

And so on January 18th 1768 Captain Horatio Whiplash watched as HMS Hesitant disappeared over the horizon. He then set about exploring the new land he had decided to settle in and since the area surrounding his settlement reminded him of home, he decided to name it New Cricklewood.

Two years later however, Captain Cook arrived and after a very bitter and ferocious game of Hide-and-Seek with

Captain Horatio Whiplash, Cook won control of the land and renamed it Australia. But that as they say, is another story!

"They are well-known for their love of fog and bright lights. So please drive carefully in wooded areas to avoid hitting any lead guitarists!"

30. The Name's Gotobed, Rob Gotobed!

In 2015 for a bet, I spent a week living in a posh London hotel not far from Hyde Park. But I wasn't a registered guest staying in a luxury room, oh, dear me no, my lovelies!

I sneaked in, then roamed the corridors illicitly, living a feral existence, sleeping in broom cupboards, feeding off scraps of food left on trolleys and giving myself the occasional all-over body wash with a discarded moist baby wipe.

I even earned a little pocket money in tips by pretending to be an elevator attendant, a shoe shine boy and a mobile masseuse. This ruse also enabled me to perform my bodily functions in the privacy of the elevator shaft, or on to empty plates left outside in the hallway. The hotel chef never did workout why so many guests left uneaten sausages on their plates!

Also, for extra kicks, I'd occasionally knock on the doors of impressionable female guests, lean towards the spyhole and announce "Hi, it's Will Ferrell!", knowing full well that everyone looks like Will Ferrell when viewed through a spyhole.

Given my ability to survive unnoticed, I'm surprised that MI5 didn't contact me with a job offer, because I clearly had what it takes to be a fully-fledged spy. The name's Gotobed, Rob Gotobed!

I'd been trained well. As a child, I was a member of the Bazooka Joe Bubblegum Secret Spy Network. In fact, I still have my codebook, my invisible ink pen, and my secret siren ring with which I could summon help if ever I found myself to be heavily outnumbered by SMERSH agents.

Also, although I do say so myself, I am kind of hot on martial arts as well! I am an expert in a form of self defence known as "**Dhaka Karachi**". I don't actually hit anyone, I just bore them into submission by reciting tedious facts about Dhaka, Bangladesh's most densely populated city.

"Just learned that babies born after May 2021 will automatically update when in Wi-Fi areas!"

31. Cricklewood: A Tourist Delight!

When Mark Twain wrote about the adventures of Tom Sawyer and Hucklebury Finn perhaps Cricklewood was not so far from his thoughts because, you see, Cricklewood is in fact an island of sorts with many adventures to be had.

Yes, Cricklewood, with its golden sandy beach, commanding castle, multi-national skyscraper, stunning scenery, awe-inspiring museum, a sensational Home Depot and a dearth of perverts.

Yes, we are the only town in the United Kingdom that can proudly boast that there is not one pervert of any kind in our town. Indeed the Anglo-Saxon name for Cricklewood is 'buttuc utan *pervertens*' or 'Land without perverts'.

Cricklewood is at the very heart of the beautiful United Kingdom. It has an annual rainfall of zero inches and basks in at least 16 hours of pure sunshine every day, exactly like you would expect if you were to travel to the sunshine state of Florida.

Cricklewood is actually an independent state situated within the greater United Kingdom. It has its own parliament and head of state, which is currently held by Queen Judi Dench, and it makes its own laws and has a different shaped steering wheel on the new Jaguar XL5 Fireball.

The peaceful beach of Cricklewood. Not a pervert in sight!

Cricklewood has over 2.6 square miles of beautiful unspoilt landscape, which includes many valleys and mountains. The highest mountain is Strawberry Tump, which has a peak that stands at a staggering 104 feet, especially when you think that Disney's Splash Mountain is only 53 feet tall! The deepest valley has a depth of 17 feet and 8 inches.

But don't just visit Cricklewood for the beautiful scenery, valleys and mountains, come and participate in our wonderful all year round entertainment. For example, our ancient Celtic festivals such as The Cricklewood Celtic Night, or The Festival Internacional do Mundo

Celta de Madrid y de Cricklewood, or our Eisteddfod Genedlaethol Cricklewood.

Or why not visit our Anglo-Saxon theatre and watch an original Anglo-Saxon play and learn of the origination of many of Rob Gotobed's jokes.

If camel riding is your thing, then boy have you come to the right town! There are over 72 independent camel riding schools situated in the Cricklewood area, and riding a camel is a delightful way to visit all 108 of the towns sightseeing attractions.

Why is camel riding so popular in Cricklewood? Well, camels were once the main means of transportation in Cricklewood, up until 1974, when they were reluctantly replaced by hot air balloons.

There are many other attractions to take advantage of at Cricklewood, as long as you are prepared to ignore the locals pointing and laughing at you and the smell of silage, which has almost gone now.

Take for example Gotobed Manor set as it is amongst the glorious Cricklewood scenery next to the town's recycling centre and sewerage works. The "shitty" garden as the locals call it, is designed by the genius Justin Little-Bieber and built by the idiot Incapability Brown, and is a fine example of a walled garden with no known entrance. Its mass of Japanese Matsu trees imported specially from a local shop are not to be sniffed at.

The best way to enter Cricklewood is via the ancient Egyptian viaduct and at once, you are aware that here is a land of happy, contented people who are all remarkably as daft as a brush.

The busy High Street is still the focal point of the town's activities. Note the quaint old stores whose frontages are covered with hand-painted graffiti, every one a rare example of native Cricklewood art.

Just around the corner from the High Street is the great Bailey Park, covering nearly half an acre, where all the local teenagers gather in the evening. This is an ideal place to study the typical Cricklewood youth and to pick up some useful local phrases and hand gestures.

Situated in the town centre is the Horatio Whiplash statue donated to the town as long ago as 2008.

To the left you will find Old Cricklewood. Time has passed by this remote corner; and so should you!

From Fothergill's Folly, Cricklewood's famous beauty spot set upon Strawberry Tump, which stands nearly eight inches above sea level, the town is spread below you in a Disneyland of glittering lights, changing all the time: red... amber... green... red and amber... red ......and then back to green.

Cricklewood market takes place every Tuesday morning which sells all manner of clothes, food and trinkets. Here you can purchase anything from a second hand steering wheel to Gotobed's Cocoa Nuts and marital aids.

There are also some charming little restaurants where you can try some of the local specialities, like the Cricklewood crunchy cockroach pasty or the Cricklewood turtle burger, both of which are best swilled down with one of our unique local surreal ales such as John Thomas' Todger.

If you are thinking of staying for a night then Cricklewood has a wide variety of accommodation to offer. A typical hotel in the town can offer a TV with up to 6 channels in every room, a radio in every room, a strange toothbrush in every room and a Wifi on every other Saturday.

Also, all our hotel rooms now have showers, and quite a few of these now have working showers too!

As is the custom in Cricklewood your gracious innkeeper will greet you every morning with a hearty breakfast of traditional local food comprising of a Burger King bacon & sausage sandwich on Monday, Wednesday and Friday, a KFC breakfast bargain bucket on Tuesday and Thursday and McDonald's Egg & Cheese Bagels on the weekend!

Finally, one of the best kept secrets, that even very few of the locals know about, is that Cricklewood offers some of the prime off-roading paradises in the United Kingdom. Sadly, you can no longer use four wheel drive trucks or motorbikes to get around the courses, due to the military curfew now in place around the town. But you can still off-road segway!

Yes, off-road segway is a great way to relax and break a collarbone or two. If you think you've done it all, think again! With huge water-filled craters, roads with huge pot-holes and countless minefields, the Cricklewood off-road segway course is one hell of a serious challenge!!

So, in conclusion, whatever your taste I am sure you will be awe struck by the sheer number of little-known architectural wonders and unique activities that Cricklewood has to offer.

Cricklewood, it's everyone's favourite destination! - Unless you already live there.

"It's not illegal to start telling a horror story when a cop shines a torch in your face, right guys?"

32. Interior: A Boardroom

A group of movie moguls are sat around a table in a meeting.

HEAD MOVIE MOGUL: Okay guys, I am fed up with just making Superhero movies. I want to hear some fresh, original and rejuvenating ideas to get people back in to our cinemas. Clive, what have you got for me?

CLIVE: What about we bring back the old Wild West custom of having someone over for dinner and then asking them to chop wood in return? We can then give them a pair of movie tickets to a film of their choice.

HEAD MOVIE MOGUL: Sounds good, Clive. Run me off a business plan and have it on my desk by 4.00pm.

JOHN: What about a roller coaster that gives kids the sex talk?

HEAD MOVIE MOGUL: Would Mickey Mouse be involved?

JOHN: No.

HEAD MOVIE MOGUL: Like it.

An intercom beeps.

SECRETARY'S VOICE: There's a Mr Gotobed to see you sir.

HEAD MOVIE MOGUL: Ah send him straight in will you.

Rob Gotobed enters the boardroom.

HEAD MOVIE MOGUL: Rob, why is there never anything good on at the cinema?

ROB: Bury me naked with a multicoloured sombrero on my head, because I want to be a fun zombie when I'm resurrected!

HEAD MOVIE MOGUL: What?

ROB: I said, bury me naked with a multicoloured sombrero on my head, because I want to be a fun zombie when I'm resurrected. .....It's an idea I have for a movie.

HEAD MOVIE MOGUL: Right, and how is that going to get people back into our cinemas?

ROB: Well it's because you guys are making all the wrong type of movies. I mean, it was a good thing Edward had scissor hands or people would've been like "Why is your name Scissorhands?" and he would be like "I don't know."

HEAD MOVIE MOGUL: What are you talking about?

ROB: Well, it's like this, I'll tell you what I've always found strange about the movie Titanic.

HEAD MOVIE MOGUL: Who mentioned the movie Titanic???

ROB: I've always thought it odd, that Rose says "I won't let go, Jack. I promise" and then lets him drop to the bottom of the ocean. Strange that? Mind you, it's just like a woman to drop you after the first date.

HEAD MOVIE MOGUL: Ah I see, you were attempting to make a joke.

ROB: And what about that movie about Abraham Lincoln. I always thought that Slash would have made a better Lincoln than Daniel Day Lewis?

HEAD MOVIE MOGUL: You mean Slash the rock guitarist?

ROB: Yeah, I mean he already had the hat!

CLIVE: *(Excited)* Oh, oh, I know an interesting 'Fun Fact' about that movie: Did you know that in order to become Abraham Lincoln, during filming, Daniel Day Lewis ate nothing but 10 inch gophers?

HEAD MOVIE MOGUL: Moving on. …..John any input?

JOHN: I always thought it tragic that Lincoln never got to play Monopoly with the top hat.

HEAD MOVIE MOGUL: Ask an idiot for his contribution and that's the type of answer you should expect. Rob, have you got anything to add?

ROB: What about? No, no, it's too radical an idea.

HEAD MOVIE MOGUL: No, go on Rob, let's hear your idea?

ROB: Well, I know they aren't ideal! But in a pinch, those oven gloves you buy at a department store actually could make pretty decent goalkeeper gloves.

HEAD MOVIE MOGUL: Tell me Rob, are you on drugs?

ROB: Why would I be sitting on drugs?

HEAD MOVIE MOGUL: I mean, have you taken any drugs?

ROB: Taken them where?

HEAD MOVIE MOGUL: I meant used drugs? `

ROB: No, I prefer new ones.

HEAD MOVIE MOGUL: Oh my god! Look Rob, where do you see yourself in five years?

ROB: Having sex on the moon.

A confused look appears on the Head Movie Mogul's face.

ROB: Hey relax, I'm kidding. ……..If I'm not there in two, I don't deserve to be in this line of business.

JOHN: You know what you don't see enough of these days?

EVERYBODY IN THE BOARDROOM: (Together) What?

JOHN: Films about superheroes.

A single gun shot is heard.

HEAD MOVIE MOGUL: What a senseless waste of life!

THEY ALL SMILE AT THE CAMERA.

End with a gradual cinema fade to an Alfred Hitchcock silhouette.

"Yes, I know the Geneva Convention was a big historic thing! But seriously, how many people named "Geneva" actually turned up?"

33. Rob Gotobed Campaign For 'Surreal Ale'

Here is an update on the Rob Gotobed campaign for 'surreal ales' which are traditional old Cricklewood beers that are unfiltered, unpasteurised, and served from non sequitur casks. They are mostly to be found in the old illogical pubs of the town.

Surrealism ales were first developed by the Gotobed family out of their Dada activities during World War 1.

The most recent addition to their exclusive collection is 'Gotobed's Stout Phallus!'

For hundred's of years, the brewers of Cricklewood have been sticking their index fingers up ducks bottoms, (nobody knows why?), this mild ale is their tipple, drinking their own urine is their topple, and there's no such thing as a Cricklewood tupple!!

The secret of this brew has been handed down in the Gotobed dynasty, from great-great-grandfather to great-grandfather, great-grandfather to grandfather, grandfather to father, father to Rob and then Rob back to great-great-grandfather who wasn't even dead, but just holding his breath.

In fact, nobody born in Cricklewood actually dies. If truth be told, they had to shoot three of the local inhabitants to start the town's first cemetery.

But I digress, this beer is best drunk from a large, buxom cleavage.

'Gotobed's Droop' is also a recent addition.

This very pale dark purple ale, is made from hops that have been carefully insulted for six months by a computer nerd in a bobble-hat. A fine ale from the North of England. It travels rather badly, and has become more popular in the South-East of England where it is used as aviation fuel.

In fact, Sir Richard Branson at Virgin Atlantic swears by it and is even rumoured to be conducting top secret tests on its formula for use with the new Virgin Galactic commercial spacecraft.

Finally, they've just added, 'John Thomas' Old Todger'. A pink ale noted for its distinctive dark yellow colour. It is made from hops that have been subjected to 'irony' from two topless Swedish barmaids, for up to three months per breast.

"Last night I misinterpreted some deer footprints in the snow and told my scout troop to look out for babies running at 40 mph!"

34. The Tokyo Comedy Store: October 2015

I completed my three gigs at The Tokyo Comedy Store this weekend and they were, as always, an unqualified success.

I arrived at The Comedy Club with my double decker tour bus, full of cheerleaders, grapes, tightrope walkers, fire-eaters and performing ex-wives at 10.00pm.

The streets were already crammed with priests, well-wishers, fans and followers. All of whom hoped to catch a glimpse of me without my make-up on.

I adjourned to my dressing-room to address myself to the task of selecting the three most desirable inflatable groupies provided for my sport.

I handed out well over a million signed photographs and 'Rob Gotobed is a terrifically exciting lover!' T-shirts.

Once inside the Comedy Club you could sense the tension and excitement that thrilled through the expectant crowd of 80,000 plus screaming fans.

Every available space inside the club was filled and outside tickets were exchanging hands for $50,000 each!

Sorry everyone, but I can't keep this ridiculous pretence up for a moment longer, and I suspect most of you knew I was making it all up anyway. And you were right!

The reality was that I arrived early, walked the wind-swept streets of Tokyo alone, and played soccer against a derelict building with an empty Yebisu beer can.

Oh, the loneliness of the long distant stand-up comedian since his excommunication from his beloved BBC.

Anyway, I just want to say thank you to EVERYONE who came to see my shows at The Tokyo Comedy Store.

You Japanese guys were FANTASTIC, thanks for being so incredible and nice. I had an AWESOME time.

Tokyo the only show where I got 800 individual standing ovations. ….One at a time, as the audience got up individually, bowed and left mid-show. - Must be a Japanese tradition I don't know about?!?

Thanks Tokyo! Hope to see you again soon.

"I know I've become a bit of a cult, because whenever I'm walking down the road I can hear people walking behind me shouting, Hey Gotobed you cult!"

35. The Rob Gotobed Stealth Condoms!

Hi! My name is Rob Gotobed and I run The Rob Gotobed Marital Aid Shop.

Today's special offer….

ROB GOTOBED STEALTH CONDOMS ONLY $9.99 PLUS TAX!

Yes, Rob Gotobed's NEW 28.5% reliable Stealth Condoms. Especially hand crafted for the considerate lover who just wants to be in and out without anyone noticing.

Yes, show her you really care!! Only $9.99 plus tax from The Rob Gotobed Marital Aid Shop!

Like the sound of those?

Then why not try Rob Gotobed's new Chinese laundry on 55th Street called R Pong!

"R Pong", I hear you say?

Yes, we are always R Pong till 11.00pm!! (I thank you!)

"Just found an ant in my trainers. He looks totally ridiculous, they're way too big for him!"

36. American Bald Eagle On American Idol!!

Of course, it used to be that everyone loved watching 'wildlife' programmes. You know the type, the ones with the cuddly penguins and the adorable meerkats. Yet I have to say that I am deeply, deeply concerned about the recent round of 'wildlife' programmes that are being transmitted in both America and Britain.

Indeed, in the light of Britain's Got Talent and Susan Boyle's continuous mental health problems, have any lessons been learned at all?

In their defence, the likes of the BBC, NBC & National Geographic will argue that every summer, they are deluged with wildlife wanting to be on their programmes.

As a National Geographic spokesman says, "One year, we had to put up a sign saying: 'No more buffalo please!!' There were a lot of disappointed buffalo that year, but it is a measure of how successful our wildlife 'reality' programmes have become and how willing most wildlife are to participate."

But is this really an excuse? Where does entertainment end and wildlife exploitation begin? Indeed as an American Bald Eagle who appeared on the American Idol show last year told us:

"You do get to like being in front of the cameras and all the attention from the public it brings. Then one day, the cameras are gone, the designer gifts and award ceremony invites dry up and you're just another reality TV has-been, who just happens to be an American Bald Eagle.

Even my chicks who were born 'live' on the actual programme, just left! And they did it without a single backward glance, which has to be hard on any father but to go through it 'live' on national TV, only added to my distress.

And did any of the major networks offer me any counselling?

Did they f**k! I was used and then dumped. I tried to get into the Betty Ford Center but they don't take bald eagles, so I had go to a local owl sanctuary for several weeks at my own expense.

I feel very bitter about my whole experience and would warn any animal against appearing on a show like 'America's Got Wildlife', and I include the Bornean Orangutans, even though they are absolutely gagging for it!!"

"My girlfriend just told me she wants a horse drawn carriage for our wedding. Well that's a joke for a start. - A horse can't hold a pencil!"

37. Rob Gotobed's Healthy Lifestyle Tips!!

In the week it was announced that eating Twinkies can give you herpes, that spending time on Twitter can lead to Hypertrichosis (the Werewolf Syndrome), that just one can of root beer can increase the risk of male impotency by 99%, and that one packet of beef flavoured potato chips can lead to Mad Cow Disease, we are pleased to introduce Rob Gotobed's Healthy Lifestyle Tips!

Yes, Dr Gotobed author of the best selling book: 'Salt - It Knows Where You Live!' has been leading the way in scaring people since 2006!

Although Rob cannot enter into individual correspondence, as this is associated with him bothering to write back, and having to find a pen. He is willing to answer any of your questions via this column, and as he says: "If, by the end, I haven't squeezed all the pleasure out of your life then I haven't done my job properly."

All of Dr Gotobed's replies are backed up by scientific-sounding evidence of the kind that doesn't bear too much close scrutiny!

"You can be sure of that!" confirmed Dr Gotobed who would also like to make it clear that he did not buy his doctorate, even though it cost him $87.76 via a correspondence course he never actually completed.

He also added, 'that living for a long time can lead to old age' and 'that flower arranging can cause your ankles to go missing.'

Anyway we are sure you will find the following Dr Gotobed handy health tips' invaluable:

1. If you feel a build-up of cholesterol then just go to the toilet. But please remember to flush afterwards.

2. Ditch the whiskers and put on your sneakers!

3. Sniff the apple if you want to avoid being a stiff in the chapel!

4. Just because you have a desk job doesn't mean you have to be sedentary. Try putting the desk on your back and taking it out to lunch with you.

5. Marijuana can count as one of your five-a-day vegetables. ***(Very important this one!)***

6. Taking out a membership with a gym or a fitness center is always a step in the right direction, but seriously, would it kill you to just eat less cookies?

7. Always bend your knees when you lift something heavy! This is for two very good reasons, firstly it protects your back from an injury, and secondly, because regrettably those leggings you wear do tend to sheer when you bend over.

Be seeing you

Dr Robert Gotobed

Dr Robert Gotobed

Rob Gotobed is the only doctor who high-five's his patients every time they drop their underpants, and shouts, "Way to go!"

**This blog was sponsored by Dr Rob Gotobed's Health Centers – 'We're ready to scare you!'

"Entering a password correctly on the third attempt is as close as I will ever get to defusing a bomb!"

38. Rob Gotobed Incorporated Shareholders Annual Report April 2022

Dear Shareholders

2021-22 has been another good year for Rob Gotobed Inc, what with the purchase of a new water bed and a new girlfriend all added to the company assets.

But I understand that in these troubled times some of you, and I emphasise only some, my cousin Wilf Gotobed has no complaints, have expressed anxiety about the performance of the companies in which I, as a so-called expert, invest on your behalf.

This anxiety was exasperated, many of you feel, by myself in a recent interview with The Wall Street Journal, where I compared the current 'Rob Gotobed' business strategy to a car wreck waiting to happen.

But let me explain. What I meant was that being men, we are unwilling to pull over in our cars and ask someone for directions. This is because this would imply that they are somehow cleverer than us. And obviously they're not, because we're toasty warm in a flash sports car and they're mooching around on foot. Many of you feel that this is not the attitude that I as your finance director, chairman and CEO should be expressing.

Firstly, I would like to point out that I have never been slow to admit my mistakes. Only last week I issued a public apology for the over-enthusiasm of my forefathers at the time of the Bengal Bubble in 1769, the Credit Crisis of 1772 and the Panic of 1873.

I also promised to repay every surviving investor the money he had lost. A pledge I was proud to report was fulfilled immediately.

By the way, I got that last piece of financial advice from Donald Trump.

That venture was the first, but to critics I would emphasise by no means the least successful, of my enterprises.

Now about Fuku Sushi Houses, Wok and Roll Chinese fast food outlets, and Gotobed's Amazing Umbrellas, well I'm sad to say they all folded. As did, through no fault of mine, the Escort Agency and massage parlour formed by the monks of Tintern Abbey.

Also, I have very little to say about my involvement in the Donald Trump School of Culture and the President Bush Course in a Wider Vocabulary.

It would be wrong to dwell only on my failures when I haven't had a single triumph. But other noticeable failures have been an expensive, but wholly patriotic attempt to impregnate the whole of Los Angeles, and the unfortunate collapse of State Secrets Limited, which made the mistake of selling its products in department stores across Russia and Iraq.

All this should, I think, reassure you that I have your best interests very much at heart.

For my own part I am now taking a longish vacation in a sheltered spot called Leavenworth Penitentiary in Kansas, but keep buying!

Be seeing you! (Hopefully)

Best wishes

Rob Gotobed

PS: Rob Gotobed is a lost cause and he's proud of it!!

"All I want from life, is to meet a woman who loves me so much that she gets my most popular tweet tattooed on her. ...Is that too much to ask?"

39. Rob Gotobed's Halloween Nightmare

This year I am proud to present a Halloween Special entitled, **'Stranger Than Pumpkin Nuggets - The Curse Of The Vampire Turtles!'** (F/X the sound of lightning)

There is no question that there is an unseen world. The problem is how far is it from my home and how late does it stay open?

How many of us have not, at one time or another, felt an ice-cold vampire turtle on the back of our throats? Not me, thank God, but some have. In fact, my girlfriend has many a time.

But what is behind these experiences? Or in front of them, for that matter?

Also, after death is it still possible to take showers? And if so, do ghosts have ray-guns?

Fortunately, these questions about psychic phenomena are answered in my soon to be published book, 'Boo To You!' In which I, Rob Gotobed, have assembled a remarkable history of supernatural incidents such as the bizarre experience of two sisters living in opposite parts of the world, one of whom took a shower while the other one mysteriously got clean.

Or the strange case of the identical twin who had a

conversation with his own reflection in a window thinking it was his brother.

Or, the bizarre story of a nine-year old Chinese girl who, while playing Dorothy in the Wizard of Oz in Songjiang near Shanghai, in July 1992 was suddenly carried off stage by a whirlwind and deposited unhurt in a treetop in Kansas. She remained there for fifteen years until her parents could raise the airfare back.

Or the even stranger case of the primary school pupil who was transformed into a llama after accepting a sweet from a stranger.

Also in the book, I explain why I believe the spirit world is more advanced than ours by approximately 25 minutes, and why ghosts 'hovering' may be a socially acceptable form of foreplay in the spirit world.

'Hovering' is indeed very pleasurable. I myself once hovered over a twenty-three year-old actress for six hours and 18 minutes, and had the best time of my life!! This has not affected me in anyway, although I can no longer converse with my girlfriend without the use of a hand puppet.

What follows is but a sample extract from chapter eight of my spooky book…

A woman who has just died is delivered to her local funeral directors wearing an expensive red dress with a matching red velvet choker.

The undertaker asks the deceased's husband how he would like the body dressed? He points out to the husband that his wife does look good in the red dress with the matching red velvet choker that she is already wearing.

The widower, however, says that he always thought his wife looked her best in a black high-neck dress, and that he wants her to be buried in one of those.

He gives the undertaker his credit card and says, "I don't care what it costs, but please have my wife in a black high-neck dress for the viewing."

The husband returns the next day.

To his delight, he finds his wife dressed in a gorgeous black high-neck dress and the dress fits her perfectly.

He says to the undertaker, "Whatever this cost, I am very impressed. You did an excellent job and I'm very grateful. How much do I owe you for the dress?"

To his astonishment, the undertaker replies, "There's no charge!"

"No, really, I must compensate you for the cost of that exquisite black dress!" he says.

"Honestly, sir," the undertaker says, "it cost nothing!"

"You see, a deceased woman of about your wife's size was brought in shortly after you left yesterday, and she was wearing a black high-neck dress.

I asked her husband if he minded his wife going to her grave wearing an expensive red dress with a matching red velvet choker instead, and he said it made no difference as long as she looked nice."

'So...

..I just switched the heads!!"

BET YOU DIDN'T SEE THAT ONE COMING!!!

And now it's time for one of Rob Gotobed's almost legendary true stories!

A couple of months ago I was staying at a hotel in the United Kingdom which was situated right opposite an old Norman church.

During the night I was awoken by a strange sound going chip, chip, chip, which was coming from the direction of the church.

The sound kept on going for a good half an hour.

So fed up, I went to complain to reception. But they said they had no idea what the sound could be and that they hadn't had any other complaints about a sound going chip, chip, chip!

I knew I wouldn't get to sleep with this sound going on, so I went to investigate.

As I crossed the road to the church I could tell that the sound was getting louder.

And then suddenly, I saw the origin of the sound!

For there, sitting cross-legged on a grave in the Church graveyard was an old man with a hammer and chisel chipping away at a gravestone.

So I went up to him and said "Oye mate, what are you doing chipping away at that gravestone in the middle of the night?"

The old gentleman slowly turned his bloodless, gaunt face around to me and said, "Don't blame me, they spelt my name wrong!"

"OMG so tired of this! For the last time, Frankincense was the name of the Wise Man who gave the gift. You're all talking about Frankincense's Gift!"

40. Rob Gotobed Is Handy Man Extraordinaire

Now I think I'm pretty good as a handyman but according to my girlfriend I'm hopeless. In fact, she would rather call in a TV repair man to change the channels on the television than let me have a go with the remote control.

Apparently, according to her, I am incredibly accident prone having already caused several major disasters in and around the house.

Although, my excuse, that I am only doing those things to demonstrate the consequences of using tools improperly, and that I plan to correct my errors as soon as I've demonstrated what can go wrong, appears to fall on deaf ears.

So, okay, the only nails I ever use are six inches long and for every job I do around the house I have to use a hammer, and that includes changing a light bulb! But, hey, I'm just your typical, average British male who loves power tools, fast cars, and even faster women.

Admittedly, most of my DIY accidents are caused by me using my power tools in what some might say is an unorthodox or in an improper manner.

My girlfriend says, it's a wonder we've got a stick of

furniture left in the house.

But to be honest, I think I was becoming addicted to doing repairs around the house. In fact, I was becoming more and more like a drug addict as I couldn't stop thinking about my next fix!

Okay, now I will admit, I did make one genuine mistake when I wallpapered our living room and used tubes of superglue to stick it up. Sixty-eight tubes of superglue to be precise!

It wasn't until my girlfriend pointed out how expensive that was, (precisely £12.99 x 68 = £883.32!!) just to put up nine rolls of wallpaper that I realised what I had done.

What made it worse was that I'd somehow managed to wallpaper the room slanting at an angle of 10 degrees towards the skirting board. The first piece had slipped by 10 degrees, and because I didn't notice I continued lining up piece after piece and continued the mistake right around the room. I thought it was funny at the time that the last piece was more triangle in shape than the others.

Mind you, it did have a peculiar affect when we had visitors as they would all gradually start to lean sideways to compensate for the wallpaper. In fact, my aunty Doreen walked around the room so much one Christmas that she was visibly seasick at the port end!

I remember another time when we had some new carpets fitted at our old house – and no, before you ask, she 'who must always be obeyed' would not allow me to fit them. But when the guys came to fit them she was at work. Anyway, once they had laid the carpets none of the doors would close properly as they were all dragging across the new thicker carpet. So the carpet fitters said, "Do you want us to cut the doors for you?" To which I replied, "Is that included in the price?"

"No", they replied its £45.00 per door.

So you can imagine my response, "No, never mind mate, I'll do it myself" Famous last words, right guys? Oh, you want to believe it!!

So, seeing as the girlfriend was still at work I borrowed my niece's 'Little Pony' six inch ruler and set to work.

I took off the living room door and then the kitchen door and estimated how much I would need to cut off. - Look, I know what you are all thinking, but hindsight is an exact science. But, I didn't know that then.

I did the living room door first, but didn't cut enough off. So it ended up still dragging along the carpet. It was dragging so much that you couldn't open the door more than a few inches, just about enough to squeeze through. So, I knew she wouldn't be happy with that, oh no!!

Disillusioned by this, I decided not to put the kitchen door back on but to use it for a picnic table instead.

The same thing happened with the bedroom door, but worst of all was when I managed to cock-up the toilet door!

For two years we never had a door on our toilet, it used to drive my girlfriend up the wall. You see the toilet was right at the top of the stairs. If a guest wanted to use it, no one could go out into the hall in case they accidentally looked up the stairs and saw another guest sitting on the toilet with their underpants around their ankles. Mind you, it would have been more embarrassing for the other guest sitting on the toilet and looking down at a stranger's face looking back at them.

I must admit on this one, I could see my girlfriend's point of view.

In fact, it was so embarrassing, I had to put a vacant/engaged sign on the inside of the living room door, which worked perfectly as long as we could all drag the door closed.

When we eventually came to sell the house I thought I had better put the door back on again. But by this time, I had lost my niece's 'Little Pony' six inch ruler. So I had to use some elastic cut out of a pair of my mum's old knickers (don't ask!).

Now, I don't know if you've ever tried to cut and measure a toilet door with some old knicker elastic but I for one would not recommend it.

In fact, I landed up sawing so much off that when I put it back on it was like a saloon door from a really low-budget Western. If truth be told, it was so bad that when you looked up the stairs from the hall and someone was using the loo, you could still see a pair of underpants around some ankles (but only this time without seeing who they belonged too!)

When prospective buyers came to view the house I used to have to use chewing gum or Blu Tack to keep the door open hoping they wouldn't notice.

But these escapades have resulted in one positive outcome! My girlfriend won't let me touch anything in our new house.

Mind you, saying that, I am attempting to perform a vasectomy on myself next Tuesday.

Be seeing you, hopefully?!?!

Is Shakespeare relevant today?!? I think the real question is, in 400 years time, will there be someone making sure people are revisiting One Direction lyrics?

And Now A Public Information Advertisement!

Have you recently spontaneously combusted?
Are you still on fire?
If so, please read this public notice carefully.

The Cricklewood Fire Brigade has to respond to over 'SIXTEEN' fires a year! So, don't waste their time by having them make unnecessary house calls when you can go to them!

If you're on fire and have suffered from spontaneous combustion within the last half an hour, please visit 'The Cricklewood Fire Station', where you will be extinguished after a short waiting period.

Thank you.

"How come whenever my girlfriend says, "we need to talk?" it's never about football or Star Wars?"

41. Fairfield Valley Psychiatric Hospital

I remember visiting the Fairfield Valley Psychiatric Hospital just before it closed in 2009. I remember the trip well, because as I was walking down this one particularly long corridor I came across an open door to a cell.

As I peered inside, I was surprised to see all these wonderful famous paintings. There was *The Dream by* HENRI ROUSSEAU, *Le Christ Jaune* by *Paul Gauguin*, The Bathers At Asnieres by *Georges Seurat*, At The Moulin Rouge by *Henri de Toulouse-Lautrec*, The Starry Night and Sunflowers by *Vincent Van Gogh* and Woman With A Parasol, Impression Sunrise and various other paintings of water *lilies by Claude Monet.*

If they were forgeries they were brilliant because as someone who has studied the originals I myself could not tell the difference. I enquired of my guide who had painted such beautiful paintings and he said they are all the work of William Billinghurst and that he would introduce me to him if I liked?

I hurriedly agreed and later that afternoon I returned with my guide to meet this William Billinghurst who was busy painting The Scream by Edvard Munch as we entered.

I said, "Mr Billinghurst I hope you don't mind me disturbing you but I am totally in awe of your work." To

153

which Mr Billinghurst replied "thank you, kind sir". I said, "any man who shows such sensitivity, patience and intrinsic quality to detail should not be incarcerated in a maximum security wing in a psychiatric hospital".

He totally agreed with me and as I spent the next two hours watching this gentlest of men create another masterpiece, I felt a real bond of friendship developing between the two of us.

So, I informed him of my decision that when I left his cell I would go straight to the Superintendent of the hospital and demand his release.

Mr Billinghurst stopped painting, put his brush down, and with noticeable tears in his eyes, stood up and he shook my hand. "Thank you sir" he said, "you do not know how much those kind words mean to me." He then sat back down again, picked up his paint brush and resumed painting.

About 10 minutes later I made my excuses and bade farewell to Mr William Billinghurst. Then together with my guide I made my way towards the Superintendent's office. I had only gone about thirty yards, when suddenly, a brick hit me in the back of the head!

I spun around immediately to be confronted by Mr Billinghurst jumping up and down shouting, "You won't forget now will you? Hey? Hey? You won't forget now will you?"

"I was 27 before I realised the girl I called sister was a puppet. My evil stepmother created her because she said I wasn't funny enough!"

42. The Legend Of King Alf's Camelot And His Knights Of The Ever So Slightly Oval Shaped Table

For many years the actual location of King Arthur's Camelot has been a mystery! However, I can now reveal for the first time anywhere, that due to a recently discovered document found in the walls of the Cricklewood Fire Station, that the exact location of Camelot was in fact on that most sacred of grounds, the Cricklewood FC football pitch.

The document also goes on to expose the true legend of King Alf, yes "Alf!" and not Arthur as we were previously ill-informed to believe.

You see, King Alf was the first good King, with the exception of Good King Wenceslas and besides his two most popular knights, Sir Galahad and Sir Lancelot, his ever so slightly oval shaped table included Sir Richard Terrapin (better known as Dick Terrapin), Sir Cumference, Sir Loin, Sir Kuss, Sir Prize and Sir Buffy the Dragon Slayer.

But out of all of his knights Sir Lancelot was King Alf's

favourite, and he never ever once got tired of hearing Sir Lancelot's favourite joke, of walking up to an innkeeper and saying, "Hello my good-man, we'd like a room for two Knights, please?"

Although it is well known that King Alf burnt the burgers at the first BBQ to be held at the Castle, it is not so well known that Sir Lancelot, the first real 'hippy' knight (he wore an old enemy's ear as an earring and also wore flared armour) liked to go skinny-dipping with the Lady of Cricklewood Lake.

This Lady of the Lake was a strange woman who was constantly seen waving one hand at passers-by. Although, allegations by Sir Galahad that she gave him the middle finger were never proved in court.

For years the Lady of Cricklewood Lake was thought to have been a cheap tourist hoax set up by the Cricklewood Town Council as a rival to Scotland's Loch Ness Monster. But what she was actually doing, by waving her hand in the air, was trying to bring someone's attention to the heavy sword she held in her other hand.

When King Alf, (Yes Alf! Get used to it!!) eventually took the magical sword 'The Exchequer' from the Lady of the Lake, Sir Lancelot was heard to call out from his sun lounger on the river bank, "Alf you Ellor!" which was a medieval term for 'you lucky, lucky blighter!'

When King Alf replied, "It was only by chance that I happened to be passing and saw her hand beckoning me",

Sir Lancelot shouted,"Then you must be the first **Chance**llor of the Exchequer!' (Groan! Groan! I thank you!)

Alf then took this sword and put it with the one he had pulled out from a stone near the Cricklewood dung heap. Please see Disney's The Sword In The Stone film for further details.

King Alf had his own personalised Wizard, known as Magic Merlin! Merlin's favourite trick was turning wine into water which he would perform every night around 11.20pm. This did not impress Alf too much, nor the flowers in his garden and the trick soon came to a stop one night after he frightened three nuns on their way home from Requiem Mass.

Merlin loved to ride a unicycle around Cricklewood and the surrounding area. But everywhere he went people always knew he was a Magician of some renown, because wherever he was and no matter what direction he was going in, he would always suddenly turn into a Castle!

He was also a wizard who enjoyed turning objects into glass – "I just wanted to make that clear!"

One of the lesser known knights of the ever so slightly oval shaped table was Sir Richard Terrapin, better known as Dick Terrapin. When this Dick first became a Knight he rode a wooden horse, but soon abandoned it when one of its wheels kept falling off!

Dick then decided to tame one of the wild stallions that roamed the highways around Cricklewood. To do this he jumped on his latest invention, 'The Poggey-Woggey', a forerunner of the pogo-stick and set off in search of a healthy thoroughbred to make his own.

Eventually he hopped onto a black horse, which he found roaming in front of The Black Bess Inn just outside Strawberry Tump. Dick named the horse, 'The White Hornet', although most of the locals thought 'Black Bess' would have been a better name.

Dick together with The White Hornet then set off on the road to becoming a living legend. (So much more fun than being a dead one!) And soon it became a regular occurrence up and down the villages of Cricklewoodshire that whenever a damsel was in distress (or that dress for that matter), or a kitten needed saving from a tree, or a camel needed taming, that the knight with the heartiest laugh and the gayest swagger would suddenly appear saying "Please reward me with some money or your wife?"

Alright, so he didn't quite get it right, which is why history has erased him out of the legend. But at least he did a roaring trade in second-hand wives in the North Cricklewoodshire area.

King Alf and his knights ruled Strawberry Tump in Cricklewood for many years. But when Alf and his knights could only get picked for the Cricklewood FC reserve team, Alf commanded Merlin to concoct a magic potion which would allow him and his knights to sleep until a time when their services would once again be required by England.

This Merlin did, allowing King Alf and his knights to achieve immortality, thus explaining why no burial site has ever been found. In fact, since those medieval days Alf and his knights have been seen on numerous occasions, mostly during their country's hour of need, with the last official sightings being during World War One and Two, and in 1966 when King Alf led England to World Cup victory at football!

So, if sometime in the future you are at the airport, when a man resembling a King with a long white beard standing next to a knight with flared armour asks you, "what time is the next flight to Brussels?" Don't laugh at him and ask what time the stag party starts? For it might be old King Alf and Sir Lancelot, off to do another good deed.

"If you can't beat them, shut off their Xbox One before your kids know they can beat you!"

Psst! Rob Gotobed's favourite joke of all time is coming soon!

43. The Top 116 Favourite Rob Gotobed Tweets

1. Did you know that in 2017 a Vincent Van Gogh painting sold for $81.3 million. All the more remarkable when you think that Vincent Van Gogh didn't sell a single painting during his lifetime. Mind you, at those prices I'm not surprised!

2. Twitter and Instagram fall out of a bar laughing about how good life is. They hear two voices begging for change; when they look down they see it's Bebo and MySpace. Twitter and Instagram quickly sober up and hail a taxi.

3. "Every time I go out, there's always someone who wants a selfie-painting with me. It's just so annoying!" - William Shakespeare c.1589

4. After the critical success of the movie 'Nomadland' which was written, produced, edited and directed by Chloé Zhao, Chloé is hoping to have similar success with her next film project: Paddington Bear Nopantsland!

5. My great-grandmother would have survived the sinking of the Titanic if she hadn't spent three hours looking for a non-smoking lifeboat.

6. Why is it that the Police never seem to like it when you ask them if they need any help? Especially when I'm dressed as Captain Funky Trunks!

7. I'll be signing books today from 2.30 pm at Macy's on 151 West 34th Street, New York. I will be there until I'm removed by their security.

8. The internet went down today so I had to spend some time with my girlfriend. She seems like a really nice girl.

9. I used to just laugh at little old ladies who stood at bus stops and yelled at buses for not stopping, but now I'm dating one.

10. Before having any surgery, always make sure your doctor can beat you at the board game Operation!

11. I played with my great-grandfather a lot when I was a child. He died before I was born, but he was such a fun guy my parents had him cremated and put his ashes in my Etch-A-Sketch.

12. Growing up, my grandmother would always feel bad when a bird slammed head first into her patio doors. Mind you, if she had really felt bad she would have moved the bird feeder table outside.

13. Here's a nice little Christmas Idea! Why not do what I do and buy all your Christmas presents when you're stoned out of your head. That way, you're just as surprised as your kids when they open their gifts.

14. I don't know who's worse, the people who sign their pets names on Christmas cards, or the pets who refuse to sign.

15. Nothing in life makes me feel more insignificant than a public toilet flushing while I'm still sitting on it.

16. Nothing sadder than playing The Beatles Eleanor Rigby on your cello while watching the girlfriend you love slowly drown in quicksand.

17. I got drunk last night and ate half of my kid's gingerbread house. Does anyone know a good gingerbread contractor?

18. Sorry I commented "not one of your best," on the Facebook photo of your third baby.

19. Every Christmas, when I see Santa Claus for the first time, I always say, "Hi Santa, how long has it been?" And he always replies, "A year!"

20. Once gain the Oscars have snubbed me in the category of "Best guy who lied about being Liam Neeson to get on a film set and then stole a catering truck" - I wouldn't mind but that's now eight years running!

21. I can never watch the final scene of Field of Dreams without thinking of my dad. I think it's because my mum says Kevin Costner might be my dad!

22. A year ago, I asked a beautiful woman if she would go on a date with me. Last night, I asked her to be my wife. ....Both times she said no!

23. Hi everyone, just to let you know I've got a book coming out soon... It's my own fault I shouldn't have ate it really.

24. Call me a romantic fool! But I still feel the best time of night is when it's just me, the moon, and my sewing machine.

25 I've been doing experiments with rats and cocaine in my science lab. One rat has started choosing it over food and two others have started a PR agency.

26. When clowns first tried to invade Great Britain nobody was really concerned. "It's just one boat", someone cried. How many could there be?", said another.

27. Tortoises always look like you just asked them to help you move house.

28. I had a dream last night that I was watching the women's tennis final at Wimbledon, and everyone was stark naked including the line judges. My mate asked me who won? I said, to be honest I didn't take much notice of the scores.

29. Look, if the litter box is only for your cat to use then you need to put a sign on it or something.

30. The bare toilet paper tube next to my open laptop tells you all you need to know about last night.

31. People in the gym walking on treadmills, you do know you can walk outside for free, right?

32. I'm pretty sure I can still do 100 push-ups. I'm only 44 and I've already done 67 of them.

33. Role playing during sex can be extremely arousing! The trouble is when something goes wrong and then you have to have a relationship talk dressed as Buzz Lightyear.

34. I've just been told that if you go to McDonald's and tell them it's your birthday, they'll ask why you're there on your birthday?

35. This afternoon I've gone to show my tattoo of my grandmother to my other grandma. I don't think it's going too well!

36. I will NEVER understand women. ....Or men. .....Or trigonometry. I also couldn't really follow the second half of the Christopher Nolan film Inception. Pineapples are weird too when you think about it.

37. Although frowned upon, it's not illegal to call someone's new baby ugly.

38. It's a real shame that Steven Spielberg never said "cut" and Harrison Ford is still running away from that giant boulder

39. Just rolled down the car window and shouted "They've caught the Loch Ness Monster!" to a crowded bus stop.

40. Apple and Microsoft might be the two smartest companies in the world, but they wouldn't be so smart if we took away all their computers.

41. Breaking news: North Korea announces successful testing of World's first contraceptive bomb!

42. By the way Carly Simon, it's not being vain if the song is really about me, right?

43. "You know, I don't think we got off on the right foot!" Me at my first date with a foot fetishist.

44. If I ever lose my girlfriend at a shopping mall, all I have to do is just start checking other girls out and 'bam' there she is yelling at me.

45. Seriously, I just hope I live long enough so that one day I can tell my grandchildren how I survived the great clown wars of 2016.

46. One of the first girls I had sex with now has an Instagram account where she reviews BiC pens.

47. What do I want on my tombstone? Pepperoni, bacon, spicy Caribbean sausage, mushrooms, grilled onions and olives. .....Thanks for asking!!

48. Went for an X-ray today. I said, "Oh my God I look terrible in this one, quick delete it and take another".

49. Just heard there's a stalker in my area, which is really weird because I stare at everyone through their windows in the evening and none of them look suspicious to me.

50. Took two diazepams with some Red Bull a few hours ago. Now I'm naked and riding a lawnmower on the roof of my local Police Station.

51. I know surveying people in front of grocery stores is annoying, but I really need to know if I look good in this thong?

52. If you lose your car keys, why not do what I do. Go to a cliff, jump off and as your life flashes before your eyes, try to spot them.

53. Remember those less fortunate than you! - Kids who graduated Hogwarts this summer are facing the worst wizard job market in living memory.

54. A fun game to play at the gym is to drag your treadmill behind someone else's, and then run with an evil grin while holding a cricket bat.

55. An Idea to pitch on Shark Tank in the USA or Dragons Den in the UK. It's an app like Grindr that let's you find a nice tree in your area to read a book under.

56. I don't like the ringtone on my phone so I put it inside my fish tank. I can't hear it anymore, but every time I get a call the fish try to tell me.

57. According to the latest research by NASA scientists, by the end of 2025, everyone in Britain will have auditioned for Britain's Got Talent.

58. I don't think the person who invented the cheese grater and the first person to stop wearing a top hat get enough recognition.

59. What a day I've had! I've just been shot at by a bank security guard just for pulling out a cordless hair dryer and trying to fix a teller's hair.

60. You know what really scares me? When you have to be nice to some psycho-schizophrenic just because he lives in your head.

61. Just held the iPhone I had for Christmas under the water till the bubbles stopped.

62. My girlfriend hates it when I give her a Christmas/birthday combination gift! But hey, that's what she gets for being born in May.

63. Why is that women want to be treated as equals and yet, many of them have such comically small feet!!

64. The British League of Pessimists were protesting outside my show in Bath last night. Mind you, I seem to manage to upset everyone. The other week I had the British League of Radical Chefs chanting, "Red wine with fish!" all the way through my show.

65. Just found £40 in my jeans. The kid in me says "Buy Nerf guns and sweets", but the adult in me says "Buy wine, Nerf guns and sweets".

66. McDonald's Big Macs and Burger King Whoppers are not real food! I just found half a one behind my car seat from about nine months ago and it looks perfect. .....Tastes fine too!

67. Remember you have to practice your tambourine every day if you want to build up a good thigh callus.

68. Today I've been sweating like a 'Fortnite' fan trying to ask a girl out on a date.

69. Stop worrying about whether the glass is half full or half empty. ....And just marvel at the fact that I managed to produce so much sweat!

70. Last night my girlfriend told me she doesn't trust me anymore! I said, "oh well, that's yet another thing you have in common with my wife".

71. If I was to get arrested, I'd ask for one tweet instead of the traditional phone call. Coz all my friends let their phones go to voicemail anyway.

72. I just want my girlfriend to love me half as much as she loves that new dress she's afraid to buy.

73. Feeling sad today! Coz I just realised that if I hadn't eaten that baby corn in 2008 it would now be teenage corn.

74. The truth is that no one actually knows how to use the memory function on a calculator.
...And we're all just too embarrassed to ask now.
(And that includes NASA scientists!!)

75. Since I've got over 80,000 followers on Twitter I've had to shave off my goatee beard for tax purposes.

76. Just bought a house next to Heathrow Airport. I'm now going to paint 'Welcome to Scotland' on my roof to confuse all the tourists about to land.

77. I would never buy a bed in the shape of a racing car, because I think they are way too flashy! But I would go for an Arabian Bedouin tent bed that comfortably sleeps eight!!

78. It maybe just me, but when you're texting someone and they text "God I'm bored!", are you thinking, "am I NOT entertaining enough for you!?!"

79. Had a weird dream that Sean Connery and Nicholas Cage kept trying to offer me their wigs, saying, "They really work Rob, we're telling you!" I replied, "Guys, I need to finish cleaning these restroom toilets or Donald Trump won't give me back my bionic leg! What does it all mean?

80. I am a very caring person you know. In fact I am so caring, I carry my 97 year old grandma downstairs every morning, just so she can cook me breakfast!

81. Appearing in front of five thousand people in New York tomorrow! ...Mind you, to be honest, I can't believe they can get that many people in one courtroom.

82. Just lost my virginity! I know, I know, it's a bloody stupid name to call a rabbit. But seriously has anyone seen it?

83. We had a team building competition at work today. And I won!

84. Just been on a bit of a vandalism spree and planted my name in tulip bulbs at all the local parks. Can't wait for Spring, that'll show them.

85. Just noticed that when I walk my legs keep going past each other but they never acknowledge each other. I suppose being British they're waiting to be introduced!

86. Busy syncing up Pink Floyd's Dark Side of the Moon to my girlfriend's contractions.

87. I swear if I read another crazy theory about how advertising is brainwashing us I'll drive a new, red Subaru BRZ equipped with the standard 2.0L, four-cylinder engine and a snappy six-speed manual transmission, straight off a cliff!

88. 90% of the British and American economies is just women giving each other useless gifts.

89. You know that little voice inside you that says nobody will ever love me? It's got to be getting that information from somewhere, right?

90. Whenever I see an old couple holding hands, I think it's nice that that old man found someone to cheat with.

91. In a duty free shop, if the bottle of Whisky is wearing a straw hat, that means quality, right guys?

92. My girlfriend and I split up because of musical differences. I had taste and she didn't!

93. If your child keeps screaming "no! no! no!" at you, put on 'Rehab' by Amy Winehouse, and boom it's now a sing-along!

94. Remember kids, that the nuclear Fusion of deuterium with tritium will create helium-4. But be warned! Helium-4 is a highly unstable non-radioactive isotope whose sub-electron structure can be disengaged by sarcasm!

95. A mate of mine is having sex with his girlfriend and her twin! I said how do you tell them apart, he said "her brother's got a goatee beard!"

96. One of my favourite childhood memories is falling asleep on the settee then waking up in bed. ....I used to think, "Wow, I can teleport!"

97. My pets hate it when I anthropomorphize them, but that's just the kind of people they are.

98. My girlfriend is now refusing to let me play the Jurassic Park theme music while we're having sex.

99. Last night we had a power cut. So I listened to podcasts on my iPhone by candlelight - just like my forefathers would have.

100. This railway bookstore has no idea I don't plan to buy a magazine. So far I've looked at four! Oh to see their faces when they learn the truth.

101. I hate it when a woman goes to shake hands and I go for a French Kiss. Always makes me think, I'm probably not going to get this job.

102. If I get an email from an AOL address I assume it's from a ghost.

103. Damn, I just remembered I left Sonic the Hedgehog on when I went to a party on New Year's Eve in 1999. That little hedgehog's probably tapping his foot like crazy.

104. I have a safety deposit box which contains some cash, two face masks, a SAS style balaclava, several passports of different nationalities and a gun. Just so that when I die, people will wonder who I really was.

105. Sorry to interrupt you scrolling down but I just wanted to say, Hi, I'm Rob Gotobed and I have personally approved this Tweet.

106. If I was a woman, I'd show so much more bra strap. #BraStrapEtiquette

107. Has your mother ever asked you to lie about your age so that her lie about HER age will seem more believable? Or do I win?

108. A little bit of rain and it's surprising how quickly everyone forgets how to drive. Just saw one guy trying to start his car with a fish.

109. Britain's unemployment figures would actually be far worse if they included people who describe themselves as podcasters.

110. Why does the line in the Christmas carol 'O Little Town of Bethlehem', "No ear may hear his coming", always remind me of Deadpool?!?

111. Saw a trailer in a cinema that ended "opening January 16th" and a guy loudly said, "Hey, that's my birthday!" and another guy shouted "happy birthday!" Great days, deep joy!

112. I joined a health club and gym in January. So far this year I've spent about £300 but I haven't lost any weight and I don't feel any fitter! Now to add insult to injury, someone tells me you have to go there!?!?

113. The next time you're in an elevator with five complete strangers turn to them and say, "If the doors open and it's Aliens, let's team up to fight them!"

114. Okay, here's a question for all you zookeepers out there. Chimpanzees, why do they still have a center parting? Are they all just stuck in the 1930s?!?!

115. Here's a thought! Before toilets were invented, were people toilet trained? Or was Napoleon constantly pooping anywhere?

116. I have 4,105 tweets and 85,400 followers. If you reduce that fraction, it means 0.05 of my tweets were written JUST FOR YOU!!

"In the end, it took 317 poison blow darts to bring down Donald Trump, and we lost many good men. But by God, the plan worked!"

And now it's time for Rob Gotobed's almost legendary favourite joke of all time!

44. Rob Gotobed's Almost Legendary Favourite Joke Of All Time

When Tarzan met Jane for the first time the conversation invariably got around to the subject of sex.

Jane says, "Tarzan, what do you do for sex?

Tarzan says, "Me, go into jungle. Find tree in jungle. Find hole in tree. Then Tarzan have way with tree!"

Jane says, "Oh, but Tarzan, wouldn't you rather this?"

And with that she rips off her leopard skin bra and panties and lies spread-eagled on the grass in front of Tarzan.

Tarzan says, "Mmm, okay!"

Then after a few seconds of looking at Jane lying on the ground in front of him, he suddenly brings up his right

foot and slams it down hard into Jane's vagina!
Jane gives out an almighty scream and says, "Tarzan, why did you do that?"

To which Tarzan replies, "Me see there's no squirrels in there first!"

"Please don't kill me!" you scream, dangling out of a window at the top of the Canton Tower. "Remember when you unfollowed me on Twitter?" I say.

45. Rob Gotobed's Top Thirty Favourite Songs About Farting!

1. You Should Be Farting by The Bee Gees

2. Farting In The Dark by Bruce Springsteen

3. Papa Don't Fart by Madonna

4. Saving All My Farts For You by Whitney Houston

5. You Make Farting Fun by Fleetwood Mac

6. No More Farts (Enough Is Enough) by Barbra Streisand & Donna Summer

7. Fart In An Elevator by Aerosmith

8. Fart It Off by Taylor Swift

9. Fart Fart All Over You (I'll Let You Have It!) by Ariana Grande

10. Farts Like Jagger by Maroon 5

11. Love the Way You Fart by Eminem & Rihanna

12. Don't Let The Fart Go Down On Me by Elton John

13. Come On Baby Light My Fart by The Doors.

14. Whole Lotta Farting Going On by Jerry Lee Lewis

15. Don't Fart So Close To Me by The Police

16. Strawberry Farts Forever by The Beatles

17. Nobody Told Me There'd Be Farts Like These, Strange Farts Indeed by John Lennon

18. When You Think I've Farted All I Can, I'm Gonna Fart Just A Little Bit More by Dr Hook

19. No, No, No, The Fart Is Mine by Michael Jackson & Paul McCartney

20. Don't Stop Fartin' by Journey

21. I Kissed A Fart by Katy Perry

22. I See A Bad Fart Rising by Creedence Clearwater Revival

23. I Feel Like A Fart Machine by James Brown

24. It's My Party And I'll Fart If I Want To by Lesley Gore

25. I'm A Fire Farter by The Prodigy

26. Fart Of The Tiger by Survivor

27. I've Had The Fart Of My Life by Bill Medley & Jennifer Warnes

28. What Makes You Fart by One Direction

29. Gonna Fart Now by Bill Conti (Theme From Rocky)

30. **Let It Go** by Idina Menzel (Theme From Frozen)

"In my opinion, if God had meant us to fly, he would have put the airports nearer the cities!"

46. My Trip To The Zoo

Have you noticed how much zoos have changed?

I went to my local zoo in Cricklewood a couple of years ago and I said, "Where are all the animals then?"

And the man said, "I don't know, this is Walmart!" So, I bought some diapers in case I ever got a baby!

But then when I got to the real zoo, I found I had spent all my money on diapers. My mum always says you can never have enough diapers!

But just then, as luck would have it, a great big rabbit came along and bit me quite badly. And its owner gave me $50 not to tell the police.

Which was another bit of luck because it just so happens that Cricklewood Zoo accepts dollars! In fact they will accept any form of currency except for the Puerto Rican gumball-bead. And I should know, because I've tried!!

So in I went, and the first thing I did was to go up to one of the zookeepers and I asked him, "What's the most interesting animal to look at?" And he said, "You can try that one over there, because he's extinct!" And he pointed to what looked like to me was an empty cage, so I went and had a look, but I couldn't see very much. So after about an hour I moved on.

I then went and bought an ice-cream which cost me 1000 rubies. I would have bought a Funnel Cake but they cost 14 Bolivian bowler hats each and unfortunately, I didn't have any of those.

Then I saw a sign which said, 'Topical Fish This Way!' So I thought great, see a few "Topical Fish" and get all the latest news.

But when I went into the building, there was just a lot of fish floating about! It was more timeless than topical!

So I went to complain to another of the zookeepers.

The zookeeper told me I'd gone into the "Tropical Fish House", not topical!!!

He then told me, that during the winter months, with all the wind and stormy weather, that sometimes some of the letters on the buildings become dislodged and fall off. And obviously the letter "R" was one of the letters that had dropped off.

So after the Topical Fish House I went to look at some performing wild cats who were performing magic tricks in a big circus tent. But unfortunately, after the main cat was taken ill all the other cats just buggered off! Apparently, he was the main performer and all the others were just copycats!

But then I came across a cage which had the legendary Mississippi White Tiger in. This was very impressive, because the only thing a Mississippi White Tiger ever eats is other Mississippi White Tigers. So, you don't ever see many of those!!

I should point out at this point, that at the time of my visit to Cricklewood Zoo, I was living at my great-great-grandfather's house who was a little bit eccentric to say the least.

He had decided to stay behind but gave me his cell phone in case he wanted to get hold of me in an emergency. This was in the nineties when cell phones were very expensive, the size of a small yacht, and not as common as they are today.

Now, what my great-great-grandfather had failed to tell me was that the ring-tone for the phone was the exact same sound as dolphins mating.

So anyway, I was in the dolphinarium watching the performing dolphins.... you're way ahead of me on this story aren't you!

At which point, my great-great-grandfather had an unfortunate accident involving the iRobot Zoomba 7600 deluxe vacuum cleaner, which had him pinned against the refrigerator and was demanding four weeks protection money in advance!

He desperately wanted to get hold of me so he started trying to ring me. But with me being in the dolphinarium, and the ring-tone being mating dolphins, I failed to recognise it.

In fact, as incredulously as this might sound, the ringtone of the sound of the dolphins mating attracted the attention of the dolphins who were performing in front of us.

Suddenly, they were all getting very aroused in the arena and suddenly all hell broke loose and the dolphins were humping everywhere, in the water, on the slides and two were even attempting a threesome with the pretty young cast member who was instructing the dolphins though their routine of tricks! It was carnage to say the least.

A good while after, I made a random phone check and I found that there was eleven missed calls on the phone from my great-great-grandfather and 452 voice messages as his situation deteriorated and got more precarious!!!

When I finally answered, my great-great-grandfather was not impressed at all. He had just returned from the hospital where he had undergone a four hour operation to have various vacuum cleaner accessories removed from his bottom! .....Without I should add, the aid of an anaesthetic!

After this incident I went to get some lunch.

Then after I had finished my lunch, there was another incident in the Atlantis Sea Aquarium, specifically at The Piranha Encounter. This was a water raft splashdown-ride that also had the characteristics of a roller coaster. The attraction takes you on an Indiana Jones theme type ride which involves real live piranhas. I know, and you think you take your life into your own hands when you ride the Smiler at Alton Towers!

The ride was going really well until we came to the inverted section where you hang upside down with your hair dangling centimetres above the live piranhas. Well, I was sat next to a young attractive lady – what are the chances of that I hear you ask? When suddenly, the ride came to a screeching halt just as we were left dangling above the piranha pit from hell! It wasn't called that, I just made that bit up. Sounds good though doesn't it? - If any representative's from Cricklewood Zoo are reading this and think the same, please get in contact as I am sure we can come to some financial arrangement.

Anyway, suddenly out of nowhere about half a dozen piranhas jump up and grab a hold of this young lady's hoody and try to pull her down into the piranha pit. Naturally, the young lady started screaming and was in a dreadful state. So calmly, after I'd taken a couple of selfies, I sprang into action.

You should have seen me fighting off the piranhas. I was punching, karate chopping, kicking, biting – yes biting! Why not? Give the piranhas a taste of their own medicine I thought!!

Anyway, eventually after a few minutes, which seemed like an eternity for this poor young, attractive lady, I managed to fight off all the piranhas and thank goodness the ride started moving again.

When we came off the ride the young lady and all the passengers could not thank me enough.

The young attractive lady then said, "I'm going to make sure that the whole of Cricklewood, and the United Kingdom, if not the world, is going to know about your heroic deeds performed here today in saving my life!! I'm the Editor with The Cricklewood Times and tomorrow morning this is going to be our lead story!" She shook my hand and was about to leave when she turned back and asked me one last question, "Incidentally, which way did you vote in the Brexit 2016 EU referendum?" She inquired.

The next day, The Cricklewood Times front page story read, 'Well known comedian Rob Gotobed, assaults SIX South American immigrants and then steals their lunch!'

Women you can't live with them! You can't live with them!!

Anyway I digress, back at the zoo I saw my old school friend Gavin Trotman, he was in trouble for putting a live humming bird in his mouth! Which wasn't very nice for the humming bird, because Gavin had just eaten a whole packet of chocolate Oreo cookies. - Certainly wasn't humming, when Gavin spat him out at lunch time, I can assure you!

Anyway, back at the zoo I thought I'd better have a look at the monkeys, after all they did evolve from us!

In fact, I have always been obsessed with monkeys ever since I was a small child. My mother used to tell me stories about a cheeky little monkey who was obsessed with bra straps and who was constantly undoing them and stealing them from unsuspecting women.

No, hang on, that was me!!! I'm getting confused, because my mother used to call me her cheeky little monkey! Sorry everyone I got a bit confused there.

So, anyway, I went along to the Monkey House. Not much of a house really, it didn't have any curtains or a front door, or anything like that.

The monkeys were in, so I was standing there looking at them, and after a while, one of the monkeys started looking at me. Then he said something to all the other monkeys, and then they all started looking at me.

Then they all came over to where I was standing, and the

Chief Monkey stuck his arm out through the cage and held out his paw. He then dropped something in my hand, and when I looked down there was 50 cents!

My mother made me write him a thank you letter the next day!!

The thing about self-isolation is that it forces you to spend time with your girlfriend. Mine seems to be really nice!

My mate phoned me up and said, "how do you both occupy the time?" I said, "We play cards!" He said, "Poker?" I said, "No, but we've had a kiss and a cuddle!"

47. NOËL COWARD XMAS IN CARDIFF 1920

This is an extract from my Christmas Show which I toured in 2007. For those of you who have never been to Wales, it is a small country with a population of around 4 million and it is a very religious country, where Chapel is King. For example, in Wales you are allowed to have sex on a Sunday as long as you do not enjoy it!!

NARRATOR: Come with us now to a clandestine meeting between two married lovers at a hotel, somewhere in Cardiff, in December 1920.

Dialogue off stage.

DAVINA: I tell you darling, there is something rather menacing about the Welsh!

NOEL: You're imaging it my darling! Just keep looking straight ahead, and don't give her any money!!

DAVINA, NOEL and a little old WELSH LADY enter stage left. NOEL is wearing a smoking jacket but no trousers, he is holding a cigarette holder.

WELSH LADY: (Strong welsh accent) Are you sure you want this room?

NOEL: Yes, one must have a balcony you know.

WELSH LADY: The other rooms are much nicer!

NOEL: No, this one will be fine. It has a beautiful view.

WELSH LADY: But all you can see is the Gas Works.

NOEL: I know, but when the moonlight catches it in a certain light, it just twinkles!

WELSH LADY: How long you been married then?

NOEL: 4 years!   **DAVINA:** 6 months!!

NOEL: 6 months! **DAVINA:** 4 years!!

WELSH LADY: You are married aren't you?

DAVINA: Oh yes.

WELSH LADY: I mean, to each other?

NOEL: Of course!!!

WELSH LADY: I think I'd better have a look at your marriage licence?

NOEL: Well, it just so happens, I have it in my pocket. There now that's settled.

WELSH LADY: Well, just a minute, I'll have to get my glasses and look at it properly!

NOEL: Fair enough.

The little old Welsh lady exits stage left.

NOEL: Ah, alone at last? Lock the door and let's get at it!

DAVINA locks the door and they embrace.

DAVINA: Jeffrey, we haven't got a marriage licence, what was that you gave her?

NOEL: My old television licence! I'm afraid the scatty mare won't know the difference.

F/X: A loud banging at the door.

WELSH LADY: (Offstage) Hey, you in there? Whatever you're doing stop it!!! Because this isn't for it!! ……………………Let me in at once?

(F/X: Door knob being turned)

NOEL: I'm afraid, I can't let you in!

WELSH LADY: Why not?

NOEL: Well, it's bit awkward; I'm taking a bath!!

WELSH LADY: But there isn't a bath in there?!?!

NOEL: I know, that's what's making it awkward!! ……..Anyway, what seems to be the problem, my good lady?

WELSH LADY: Give me a TV licence you have?

NOEL: Well, I expect I left my marriage licence at home.

WELSH LADY: Well, I'll let it go this time, but I don't want no trouble see, this is a respectable house, you're not in Swansea now, you know!!

NOEL: Good, she's gone!! Well, hello there you little fox?

DAVINA: Oh and what are you after young man?

She leans forward revealing her heaving bosom.

NOEL: Well two things come to mind!

DAVINA: (She dramatically walks across the stage) Oh Jeffrey, don't you find Wales so romantic?

NOEL: I'm not sure?!? I find all that blubber gets in the way!!?

DAVINA: (She turns to face NOEL) Oh darling, wouldn't you like to rest your head on my lap?

NOEL: Well, if you can get it off, why not?!?

DAVINA turns in a dramatic gesture and holds both of NOEL's hands.

DAVINA: Oh Jeffrey, don't you just love Christmas, I know I do!!

NOEL: Oh yes, I just can't wait to get my Norwegian Spruce up, you know! **(pause)** And then to get my balls out. **(pause)** Give them a good dusting off. **(pause)** And then hang them, neatly in a row!!!! **(NOEL looks perplexed at audience)** You know Davina, I think this audience are making their own jokes up!!

DAVINA: Jeffrey?

NOEL: Yes, Da-vin-a???

DAVINA: Do you love Christmas?

NOEL: Oh yes, I love Christmas, Da-vin-a???

DAVINA: (She turns to face NOEL and beckons him closer) Tell me Jeffrey, what do you love 'best' about Christmas?

NOEL: Oh, I think you know?!?!

DAVINA: Yes **(Her eyes look down)** I know.

NOEL: (Roll eyes) I know, you know.

DAVINA: Yes, I know that you know, that I know!!

NOEL: Ah yes, I know!

DAVINA: Oh Jeffrey, I so want to make you happy. How? How can I make you happy?

NOEL: Oh I think you know. **(He falls backwards on to the couch)**

DAVINA: Yes I know, I know. **(Then a deep voice with quivering lips)** Kiss me Jeffrey, kiss me like you've never kissed another woman before. **(NOEL and DAVINA run in a big semi-circle in opposite directions and then mime a big smack of a kiss. They then touch hands and each raises their right leg)** Oooh!! **(DAVINA swoons back and fore the stage and feels faint).**

DAVINA: Tell me, does your wife suspect anything?

NOEL: No! She thinks I'm playing 'Charley's Aunt', at the London Palladium!!

DAVINA: (Giggles)

NOEL: Oh, it tickles you does it? Oh how I love to hear you laugh, **(Spoken in a butch voice)** Da-Vin-A!!! Oh, if only this could go on forever. Marry me?!?

DAVINA: Yes, I wish we could get married, but I'm afraid, I'm married already, and it would be bigamy!

NOEL: (Like Groucho Marx) Yes and it would be big-of-me-too!

DAVINA: You know I'm beginning to like you very much. Come, join me on the veranda!! I only wish we had some music.

NOEL: That's easily arranged. **(HE clicks his fingers and some romantic music starts)**

DAVINA: Oh Jeffrey? **(They hold hands)**

NOEL: Oh Davina?

DAVINA: Oh Jeffrey? **(Slightly deeper voice)**

NOEL: Oh Davina? **(Slightly deeper voice)**

DAVINA: (In a really deep voice) Oh Jeffrey?

NOEL: (In a very deep voice) Oh, Da-Vin-A?

DAVINA: (In a mega deep voice) So do you want to get this dirty weekend in Cardiff started?!?!

NOEL: (In a feminine voice) Not half!!

They embrace And kiss.

STAGE LIGHTS GO OUT. STAGE IS NOW DARK

NARRATOR: Come with us now to another part of Wales. It's Christmas morning, the year is 1868, and the small welsh mining community of Trigelli is in the grip of the coldest winter in history.

F/X wind blowing.

VOICE: And how cold is that exactly?

NARRATOR: Well, see that brass monkey over there?

VOICE: Yes?!?!

F/X: Two large metal balls falling to the ground.

VOICE: Ooooh, that is cold!!

Stage lights go up on an interior of a small Welsh mining cottage.

NARRATOR: Come with us now, as we present, 'How Green Was My Lettuce'.....

MEGAN and the local doctor are huddled around a sick DAI in bed.

MEGAN: So, what do you think then doctor?

DOCTOR: Well, this bed cover doesn't go with those curtains. **(Then to audience)** I'm completely mad I am!!

MEGAN: I mean about Dai?

DOCTOR: Oh Dai's got a nasty case of 'Sticky Mattress'!?!?

MEGAN: Dai's got a nasty case of 'Sticky Mattress'!?!?

DAI: (His eyes suddenly opening) Well it beats working!! Hee-eee-eee!

MEGAN: Isn't there anything you can do doctor?

DOCTOR: No, I'm afraid I've carried out every medical test known to the Trigelli Male Voice Choir.

MEGAN: Oh, then it's curtains for him!

DOCTOR: No it's a bed cover I told you! **(To audience)** I told you I was mad see!! **(He laughs)**.

MEGAN: Oh doctor, but when I see that little 'dwt' sleeping, all cwtched up in bed, dew, dew, I could eat 'im!

DOCTOR: (Raises his voice) Megan!!!!!! I hope not!!! Not, without adding some slimline vinegar dressing first!! **(To audience)** Completely barmy, what did I tell you!?!?

Carol singing is heard off stage.

MORRIS: (Runs onto the stage) Mam! Mam!!

MEGAN: What is it Morris minor?

MORRIS: Mam, there's a carol singer outside? Oh hello Dr Trevor, I didn't recognise you with your clothes on!

DOCTOR: (To audience) Well, what can I tell you? I like to practice in the nude!!!
(He pulls some pervy faces to the audience).

MEGAN: Now be a good girl, and go and answer the door our Morris?

MORRIS goes to stage right and opens an imaginary door to find a carol singer standing there.

MORRIS: Who are you?

ROB: I'm a poor carol singer!

MORRIS: Two pennies?

ROB: I've only got one?!?

MORRIS: That'll do! **(He snatches the penny out of ROB's hand)** Thanks very much!?!? **(ROB milks audience with sad face to get them to go "arrr!!!")** Well, what are you waiting for? Sod off!! **(Slowly ROB turns and slowly starts to trundle off stage).**

MEGAN: Morris? Who was that at the door?

MORRIS: Some 'idiot' singing carols. He gave me a penny!!

DOCTOR: He gave you a penny! You're supposed to pay him, you dummy!! **(To audience)** Let this serve as a warning to all parents, and especially those with children!!

MEGAN: Ah, the poor man we can't leave him outside in the cold wind and snow. **(She goes after ROB and stops him)** Sir? Sir?? Aven't you got anywhere to be on Christmas morning?

ROB: No, I haven't! I haven't got anybody! I'm all alone, you see. **(To audience)** Nobody loves me! Nobody cares about me!!

MEGAN: You come in, and 'av a warm by our fire? **(She helps ROB over to the fire)** Ah, that's better than being out in the cold wind and snow, isn't it? This is my son Morris. Morris go get the nice man a drink and a slice of lava bread.

ROB: I don't want to be a nuisance?

DOCTOR: Then get lost, so we can carry on with our traditional Welsh Christmas! **(He grabs MEGAN)** Can't you tell how much I love you Megan? **(He starts snogging her, and gnawing at her like a dog).**

MEGAN: (Trying to ignore the DOCTOR's advances) Ah, but the poor man looks half starved. What have we got left to give him?

ROB: That shrivelled lettuce, looks crisp, and green and even.

MORRIS: That's not a lettuce, that's the turkey!

MEGAN: Have one of my home-made Christmas cookies?

DOCTOR: Aye, if you gotta go, that's as good a 'way' as any!! **(DOCTOR and MORRIS both laugh)**

MEGAN: Morris, fetch the gentleman some cheese?

MORRIS: Right! 'Ere mousy, mousy, mousy??? **(MORRIS takes some cheese off a plate on the floor)**

MEGAN: Morris, please show our guest a bit of compassion**?**

ROB: It's nice to see a family spending a traditional Christmas all together!

MEGAN: Oh, do you want to see what they bought me for Christmas? I had these beads. **(She grabs her throat)** Oooh, the beads have broken!!

DOCTOR: I thought the gravy was lumpy!!

MEGAN: Doctor give the fire a poke?

DOCTOR: But it's electric!!

MEGAN: I know! Right, let's have some Christmas festivities. Morris? Nuts?

MORRIS: I don't care. I'm happy!!

MEGAN: Doctor? Crackers?

DOCTOR: I don't care. I'm happy!!

MEGAN: No, I meant have you got the crackers?

DOCTOR: No, it's just the way I walk!

MEGAN: Enough of the cracker jokes. I'm talking about the thing you put in your hand and pull?

DOCTOR: Well, I've got one of those, but I'm not going to stick it on the table!!

MEGAN: (Raising her voice) Will someone please pull a cracker with this man?

ROB: Oh, it's all very jolly and festive?

MORRIS: Pull? Hey there's a joke in this. It says, what did Cinderella say when her photos from the ball didn't arrive?

DOCTOR: I don't know, what did Cinderella say when her photos from the ball didn't arrive?

MORRIS: "One day my prints will come!"

ROB: Oh, this is the nicest Christmas I've ever had. But I am very sorry, I must be on my way.

MEGAN: Morris, Doctor, we can't let the poor man go out in the cold, all alone on Christmas day.

ROB: Ah, but you see I'm not a poor old man really.... **(Pulling off his cloak to reveal he is in fact a millionaire)** I'm Rob Gotobed and I am an eccentric millionaire!?!?

MORRIS: Hey everyone, he's an electric millionaire!!

ROB: No, I am not an electric millionaire Morris. I'm an "eccentric" millionaire!! And I am going to grant your family a Christmas wish for being so kind to me.

MORRIS: See, I knew he was a pervert! I bet his Christmas wish involves us dressing up in lederhosen and slapping each other on the thighs with wet kippers.

MEGAN: Shut up Morris, and let the gentleman speak.

ROB: No what I mean, is that for the first time in my life, I have found real warmth, compassion and understanding. I think you are the kindest people I've ever met, and so in return I want to grant you a Christmas wish that I will make come true!!

MORRIS: Oh good we're going to be rich? **(The DOCTOR's eyes light up and he puts his arm around MEGAN as she lights up her pipe).**

MEGAN: (Taking the DOCTOR's arm off her shoulders) No, it's alright Mr Gotobed, but like I've always said, 'Money doesn't buy you wealth!!"

DAI: (His eyes suddenly opening) That is very true and profound our Megan. It's like I always say, "it is only the hairs on a gooseberry, that stop it from being a grape!!"

ROB: Ok fine, I understand, but thank you for restoring my faith in humanity. **(He goes to leave but then stops)** Oh, one thing before I go?

ALL: (They all lean forward) Yes?

ROB: Can I have my penny back?

The cast freeze.

GRAMS: Christmas music starts up and the stage lights go down.

The End.

48. Scientists Don't Want You To Know That Our Earth Is Really A Giant Oreo Cookie!

Yes, we've all heard of conspiracy theories, whether it was that Paul McCartney died in 1966 and was replaced with a lookalike, or that Prince Charles is a vampire! The latter theory gains credence because according to the genealogy records, Prince Charles is descended from Vlad the Impaler who was the inspiration behind Bram Stoker's Dracula. The Prince even appeared in a Romania tourism advert where he proudly stated that "Transylvania is in my blood!" - You could not make it up!

It is also widely believed that the current year is actually 1719 and not 2016! This is because basically 297 years of our history didn't exist! Yes conspiracy theorists believe that all the events from 614 to 911 have been faked, and that includes the entire Carolingian Renaissance and the figure of Charlemagne. One of the main reasons behind this theory is the scarcity of archaeological evidence from that period of time.

Also, did you know that North Korea is using 'Pokémon Go' to spy on the USA? Well it's true!

Now as readers of my fine body of works will know, I have my own original conspiracy theories that I have championed for many years. They are, that it was in fact Adolf Hitler, with the aid of a time machine, who assassinated Abraham Lincoln and not John Wilkes Booth and that the entire universe and all of our memories were only created a week last Wednesday.

Also, that NASA have photographic evidence that a German U-boat was discovered on the moon in 1969!

This last particular conspiracy theory leads me nicely on to what I really want to talk to you about today.

You see, sometimes boring, only slightly crazy conspiracy theories just aren't enough for certain people. Going above and beyond the usual 'fake Moon landings' proposition, there is a small group of people that are totally convinced that the entire Moon is a fabrication and does not actually exist!!!

Now I believe that the moon is real, but I do have my own personal reasons for believing that certain things about the moon landings were FAKED!!

As everyone knows, or in fact should know, I love America! I am fascinated by the people, the history and the geography! I have been to America many times and have always found it a worthwhile stimulating experience. But nowhere, including America, can justify travelling distances and flight times like eleven hours to Los Angeles, nine hours to Florida and seven hours to New York!

To me it makes more sense to be in an airplane for about ninety minutes and to visit somewhere like Amsterdam or Paris. I hate flying, and not for the reasons you would normally think - I hate not being in control! Which means I want to be flying the airplane and since I'm not qualified that is never going to happen!

Also, I get bored when flying for more than an hour and a half even with all the in-flight entertainment now available.

Nothing can be worse than going on a long haul flight for 15 to 20 hours only to find the place you get to is a bit crap!

I mean, after all their training and preparation, I bet Neil Armstrong, Buzz Aldrin and Michael Collins must have secretly been a bit gutted when they got to the moon and discovered not only was it not made of cheese, but to see that there was not much to do there and that it was in fact, a bit shit!

"You know when I was a kid we didn't have emojis, we had to pull a face ourselves!"

49. Jimmy The Sperm!

Once upon a time there was a little sperm called Jimmy who was known throughout the Milky Way Galaxy as Jimmy the Sperm!!

Now Jimmy the Sperm was just one of over 500 million sperms who lived in the Big Testicle of life. And in Jimmy's universe the only thing that really mattered was being the first up the Fallopian tube to fertilise an egg!

So Jimmy prided himself on his fitness, and unlike all the other sperms who just liked to go out partying and drinking every night, Jimmy preferred to go to his local gym for a good healthy workout.

Now I do admit, it does help this story if you can imagine a little sperm travelling back and fore to the gym! Obviously, I haven't completely thought this part of the story through yet – but please bare with me!

What's that reader?

No, he didn't cycle back and fore to the gym!!!

Who's ever heard of a sperm riding a bicycle? Where is the gritty reality in that?

Anyway, like I said, Jimmy preferred to go to his local gym instead of going out on the "piss" with all the other little sperms. (If you can pardon the connotations that image conjures up!)

And whenever the other little sperms taunted him to go out with them, Jimmy would always reply the same way, "No you guys go ahead, I'm going to keep on training, because when the time comes for us to enter that Fallopian tube, I'm going to be the fittest and the strongest, so that I will be the one who fertilises the egg!"

Now, why Jimmy the Sperm should talk with a Hungarian accent I have no idea!!

Anyway, this routine went on for several months. But when the eventual day came for the sperms to enter that tube – do you know who was swimming right out in front ladies and gentlemen?

Yes, that's right children, Jimmy the Sperm!!!!

Now to be honest most of the other sperms were not taking the race too seriously! In fact, most of the other sperms were racing in fancy dress! And the whole event looked more like the New York marathon.

In truth, Jimmy had already passed an inflatable Donald Trump, two Finding Nemos, three Teletubbies and eighteen Olafs to get into the lead.

But now that Jimmy was in the lead, Jimmy was swimming faster and faster, and stronger and stronger and had already increased his overall lead to well over 2.6 seconds!!

I mean, let's be honest, Jimmy was the Mo Farah of the Sperm World!

But then just as Jimmy was beginning to look invincible and with a commanding lead of nearly 5 seconds, Jimmy came to an abrupt halt!!

Then with a look of anguish upon his face, he turned to all the other little sperms swimming behind him, and said,...... and I quote!

"Quick turn back boys, we're in the poop!!

(And I cleaned this one up!!!)

So it just goes to show you, that whenever you think success is always within one last grasp – the poop is always stacked against you!!

My name's Rob Gotobed, thank you and goodnight!!

Please like me?

"The worst place to be stung by bees is at a nightclub because it just looks like you're doing some very cool dance moves. Oh sure, you win the dance competition but at what cost!"

50. Rob Gotobed - An Author's Apology 2022

Over the previous fifty chapters, and indeed throughout my entire career, I have "allegedly" posted some "inappropriate" blogs, articles and pictures.

This was never my intention!

What I thought I had written was some sophisticated, intelligent and cerebral material to entertain you my beautiful, cosmopolitan, suave, debonair and enlightened readers, who I thought shared the same sense of humour as myself.

Unfortunately, this wasn't the case and since I published this book it would appear that I seem to have upset quite a few more people who have accused me of being rather shallow and in some cases even, dare I say it, sexist!

If you were one of these people who thought this, please accept my sincerest apologies.

Looking to 2023 and onward, I will only post blogs, articles and pictures of a cultural, educational or informative subject matter, such as in reference to old historical monuments, castles, churches and penguins.

On the next page is a picture of the Castle Gate Bridge in Cricklewood. It is the oldest bridge in Cricklewood and indeed England and it took over two hundred years to build. It was completed in 1642.

Cricklewood bridge in England. The only remaining fortified river bridge with a gate tower in the United Kingdom.

The Fake End.

If you or a friend have been affected by any of these short stories and are in need of some counselling? Or, if you have any questions, please give Rob Gotobed a call on 01 0800-FakeCelebrity, the number one premium phone service for fake celebrity discussions of a vague, one-size-fits-all nature!

And finally, an update on the world credit crisis: The British pound had another good day yesterday! It got out of bed just after 10.00am, had pancakes with maple syrup for breakfast and then went for a nice walk in the countryside. This contrasts with last week when the pound closed at only 2.4 against the Oompa Loompa Bugle Bead of Company B!.

BREAKING NEWS: Pope ends ban on contraception, and pays an unexpected visit to Florence!

No Publishers were hurt during the making of this book

The Real End.

BONUS*BONUS****BONUS****BONUS****

And now, especially for the purchasers of the Deluxe, Executive version of this Rob Gotobed book, here is the legendary lost script for his BBC pilot comedy.

51. The Magnificent Moodies!

Written By: Rob Gotobed

List of characters in order of height:

ROB: A twenty something author. The word author is loosely used as he has been writing the same, as yet unpublished, book since the age of 12. He owns 'Moody Books' a book shop situated on Cricklewood High Street which sells antiquarian, rare and collectable books.

He started the book shop with the money he was left by a wealthy uncle.

The extent of the amount of money that was left to Rob allows him to generally be completely indifferent to what goes on in his friends lives. In fact he sees their misery as merely an entertaining distraction, as well as an opportunity for some enjoyment.

He has a wicked but harmless sense of humor and often takes the proverbial piss out of his friends in a harmless jovial manner.

JAKE: A twenty something man who looks a lot older! He is one of the most inept and unlucky people you are ever likely to meet and is consequently a frequent target of bullies. He works as an enforcement officer for the UK Health and Safety Executive.

He is constantly vexed with impossible questions about the emptiness of human existence. He is moderately intelligent, but he makes up for this by being neurotic, self-loathing, depressed and dominated by an endless stream of female partners.

LACEY: A twenty something female who is normally intelligent and assertive, but can also be quite superficial. She is treated by Rob, Jake and Marcus as 'one of the boys' and is a keen and active member of their little gang.

Despite all the 'situations' the group get themselves into, she remains the closest female friend to the three main male members of the cast. Lacey has a tendency to get angry very easily, and has a habit of hugging people when displaying extreme emotion.

MARCUS: A forty something, unemployed dreamer from Cricklewood. A self-proclaimed eco-warrior and business guru who aspires to be like his hero Steve Jobs. However, as a result of being thoroughly disorganised, his chances range from slim to none. In reality, he is an unemployed hippy and petty criminal whose plans fail through his apathy and ineptitude. He is never seen without his beloved afghan coat.

HONEYBUN: Age unknown, is a woman of unknown Eastern European origin. She speaks in a weird Eastern European non-defined language and dresses and looks like Kate Bush in her younger days.

MR. BLUETT: A typical Supermarket department manager who always wears a suit and tie.

1   EXT. RAILWAY STATION PLATFORM - DAY   1

A sad-looking JAKE is sat at a railway station staring into space.

A train arrives at the platform he is sitting at. The guard's door opens right in front of him and without looking the GUARD empties an ice-bucket of dirty, freezing water all over JAKE.

>   GUARD
> Sorry mate.

>   JAKE
> Don't worry about it, it was bound to
> happen sooner or later.

The GUARD gets back on the train and signals for the driver to leave. The train departs, the passengers that have disembarked leave. JAKE stays staring into space.

2   INT.   A SUPERMARKET CAFE - DAY   2

LACEY and MR. BLUETT standing behind the counter are toasting with lemonade.

MR. BLUETT
To your promotion.

They both take a drink.

LACEY
Mmm, oh thank you Mr Bluett, nice lemonade.

MR. BLUETT
Ah yes, Vintage 2020. Only the best for you Lacey.

LACEY
You know, I can't tell you how much I appreciate this promotion. I mean, of course I deserve it.

MR. BLUETT & LACEY Laugh.

MR. BLUETT
Well, you're truly on your way now.

LACEY
I know, who would have believed when I dropped out of University, that one day, I would become a Counter Service Assistant at Saferose?

MR. BLUETT
Ahhh, your lecturers won't be laughing now.

A bemused expression appears on LACEY's face.

LACEY
Noooooo.

LACEY walks out into the main Café. ROB is sat at a table by himself feeling his chin.

ROB
Good shave today...

LACEY walks past ROB, stops and examines her legs.

LACEY
Yeah, not bad I suppose.

LACEY then speaks in a smug trying to impress manner to ROB.

Just got a promotion!

ROB
Wow! Impressive! What are you now Lacey? Chief bottle washer upper?

LACEY makes a false laugh and acts out that she is tying her ribs together because ROB's remark is so funny.

LACEY
Ha ha! Ha ha!! Ha ha!!!

ROB
So go on, tell us what you are?

LACEY lifts ROB out of his seat by the shirt collar.

LACEY
Listen here smart-arse, perhaps I should tell you what you are first.

MR BLUETT walks past wagging a finger towards LACEY.

> **MR. BLUETT**
> Lacy, one should never attack a customer! It's "bad" customer service.

MR BLUETT carries on walking past.

> **LACEY**
> Sorry Mr Bluett, won't happen again.

> **ROB**
> **(mimicking Lacey).**
> Sorry Mr Bluett, won't happen again. So seriously, what have you been promoted to?

> **LACEY**
> **(embarrassed)**
> Counter Service Assistant.

ROB
Woo-hoo!?!?

(changing the subject)

I'm thinking of growing a goatee. Make me look more intellectual. Like a University Professor.

LACEY groans and walks off to collect some dirty dishes.

JAKE enters the café and sits at ROB's table but does not make eye contact with him.

JAKE
I went to the railway station.

ROB
Oh, the railway station.....

JAKE
I like the railway station, ... it helps me to ....forget.

> **ROB**
> Joy Division, Unknown Pleasures type of day?

> **JAKE**
> Oh big time!

> **ROB**
> (addresses the café customers)
> Does anybody have a Valium my friend could have?

> **JAKE**
> Very funny.

Suddenly JAKE is hit by about five Valium tablets.

> Who threw those?

JAKE acts annoyed then he carefully picks the tablets up and puts them safe in his jacket pocket.

ROB
You know, I have never truly understood your fascination with
....."the railway station".

JAKE
You see Rob, it's my happy place. My great-grandfather worked for forty-five years on that railway line and do you know what they gave him when he retired?

ROB
A clock!

JAKE is not listening to ROB.

JAKE
A clock! Forty-five years he laboured on that railway line, and even on the day he retired, aged sixty-five, they made him go and carry a great big anvil from the work sheds all the way to the signal box just so the station master could straighten his fork. A fork Rob!!

ROB

A fork.

JAKE

A fork!

ROB

A fork!!

JAKE

A fork!!!

ROB

You know, I don't know why you go there? You go there whenever you're depressed, and you come back even more depressed than when you went. Every time the ticket clerk sees you coming she puts The Samaritans on red alert.

JAKE

Uh, it helps cheer me up.

ROB

No, it doesn't.

JAKE
No, you're right.

Suddenly JAKE is hit by several more Valium.

Hey, will you lay-off with the Valium!

ROB
Hey guys, give him a break.

ROB mouths "thank you, thank you" to the customers as he puts his thumb up and points to the tablets

LACEY approaches the table.

LACEY
What's the matter with Smiler?

ROB
Oh, he's depressed.

LACEY
Steps back in amazement. Wow, that's a first.

ROB
Hey, this will cheer you up. Lacey got a promotion.

LACEY
Oh, get a life Rob!

LACEY walks off to attend to some other business.

JAKE
Nice.

ROB
So, what's upset you this time?

JAKE
Rebecca phoned me earlier, and said …."I think we need to have a chat!"

JAKE virtually spits the word "chat" out.

ROB takes a sharp intake of breath.

ROB
Ouch!

                    JAKE
I know, the worst thing any girl can say to you.

                    ROB
Well, apart from 'why are you wearing my panties?'

Both JAKE and ROB high five and giggle like little naughty school boys.

So how has it come to this?

                    JAKE
Well, last night, as we were leaving the cinema... we were just kind of standing there, I noticed she was sort of smiling at me and, I wasn't sure if she wanted me to start the conversation or ...

JAKE shrugs his shoulders.

                    ROB
If she had wind?

                    JAKE
Why'd you do that?

                    ROB
What?

                    JAKE
Say something like that, whenever I try to talk to you about Rebecca?

                    ROB
I do not.

                    JAKE
You do.

                    ROB
Oh okay, I do.

ROB tries to hide a smile.

                    Sorry, look I promise I won't say another word.

ROB mimes locking his lips together and throwing away the key.

> **JAKE**
> Anyway we're standing outside the cinema when this dog comes up to me and starts barking. So she says why is that dog barking at you?
> And I said, "I don't know, I don't speak doggy!" Which I thought was quite amusing. And then she says, I think we should start seeing other people.

> **ROB**
> Whoa!

> **JAKE**
> So I said, well at least allow me to pay for your taxi home.

> **ROB**
> A kind thought.

> **JAKE**
> And then, as I go to get a twenty out of my pocket,..... a butt plug comes flying out of my jacket pocket and catches her in the face.

ROB
Yikes!

JAKE
Yes, yikes exactly.

ROB
Now obviously a certain question arises here which needs a very
careful thought provoking answer.

JAKE
Don't ask. It's a loooooong story.

ROB
So I take it it wasn't yours?

JAKE
No…. it's my mum's!!

ROB grimaces..

ROB
Alphonso!?!?

A sinister grin appears on ROB's face.

JAKE picks up some spaghetti off ROB's plate and starts eating it.

>   **JAKE**
> Mmm, nice spaghetti.

>   **ROB**
> Yeah, I thought so too until just now.

ROB drops his fork down on to his plate in disgust.

LACEY approaches JAKE.

>   **LACEY**
> Is that your shopping bag on the floor?

>   **JAKE**
> Yes.

>   **LACEY**
> Could you move it in case somebody trips over it?

LACEY moves on to clean another table.

JAKE
(extremely agitated)
Health and safety gone mad!

ROB
But you work for Health and Safety?

ROB
But you work for Health and Safety?

JAKE
(extremely agitated)
I know, you don't have to keep reminding me.

JAKE picks up his carrier bag and places it on the empty chair next to him.

ROB
What's in the bag?

JAKE
The usual. Chicken nuggets, beef burgers, chips.

ROB
Don't you cook anything but frozen food?

JAKE
Who's got time to cook them? I just suck them frozen.

ROB
Another culinary disaster?

JAKE
Oh yes! ......Oh yes!!

ROB
Go on, what happened?

JAKE
Well, I wanted to cook something to impress my mother and her 'NEW' boyfriend.

ROB
You mean…. Alfonso?!?!

A sinister grin appears on ROB's face.

JAKE
(extremely agitated)
Yes, …..

JAKE has to stop himself from adding an expletive.

**** Alfonso!

ROB
Go on.

JAKE
I got all the ingredients, but I was running short of time. So, basically, I tried to make a Lobster Bhuna in the pressure cooker.

ROB
How did it taste?

                    JAKE
            I don't know, it's still on the
            ceiling.

3   EXT.   A HIGH STREET - DAY   3

ROB and JAKE are walking down the street.

                    ROB
            So, she walked in and caught you
            red-handed, so to speak?

                    JAKE
            Yep! It was the single most
            damaging experience of my life.
            ….Well, apart from seeing my
            great-grandfather naked! So, tell
            me about this girl you met the
            other night?

                    ROB
            Oh Vicky she's great. She's a lawyer.

JAKE
So how old is she? Nineteen, twenty?

ROB
Ah .....forty-two.

JAKE
Forty-two!! Have you taken leave of your senses?

ROB
No, we're fine.

JAKE
Wow! But forty-two!! Are you sure?

ROB
I'm pretty sure although I haven't chopped her in half and counted her rings yet.

JAKE
Wow! Forty-two that's old!!

ROB
I know. I can handle it.

JAKE
So, do you need that K-Y Jelly stuff?

ROB
No.

JAKE
Okay.

MARCUS appears on the opposite side of the street, walking in the same direction, he is wearing an old Afghan coat. He spots ROB and JAKE and dramatically tries to get their attention.

MARCUS
Oye!

MARCUS whistles to get their attention.

ROB
Hey there's Marcus.

ROB points out MARCUS to JAKE and shouts across the street.

Hey Eric?

JAKE
Rob, there's something I've always wanted to know. Why does everyone call Marcus, Eric?

ROB
Because he looks like Eric Cantona.

JAKE
He looks nothing like Eric Cantona.

ROB
I know.

ROB shouts across the road to MARCUS.

Hey Eric?

MARCUS
Hey wait there.

MARCUS then proceeds to run across the road causing cars in both directions to screech to a halt. He confronts one annoyed driver.

Back off mate! I'm an ex-Para! Never! Never!! Try to run over an ex-Para, ...bandsman who hasn't cleaned his trumpet yet.

MARCUS makes it across the street to where ROB and JAKE are standing.

MARCUS
I'm glad I ran into you two.

Another annoyed driver toots his horn at MARCUS as he drives off. MARCUS responds to the driver with some bizarre unknown hand gestures.

I wanted to tell you that I'm going to be away on business for a while.

JAKE raises his arm and makes a sound like a buzzer.

> **JAKE**
> Ah? Excuse me, what business?

> **MARCUS**
> Business! I have business… and clients, and stationery, and things. Tell him Rob!!!

> **ROB**
> Yeah, he has business, lots of business, BIG business!

Then as an aside to MARCUS.

> What type of business you in?

MARCUS laughs and makes a mock gesture to ROB's face with his fist.

> **MARCUS**
> Ha ha! What is this guy like? Nice one Rob.

> **ROB**
> **(sudden realisation)**
> It's not the Quicky Licky Ice Cream Company again?

MARCUS spins around 360 degrees.

> **MARCUS**
> Shush!!

MARCUS then looks all around them secretively.

> I told you to forget all about The Quicky Licky Ice Cream Company.

> **ROB**
> Is it a personality disorder, bad karma or sheer rotten luck that allows me to have friends like you two?

> **MARCUS**
> **(starts coughing and choking)**
> Where are you guys heading?

                    JAKE
To the launderette.

                    MARCUS
Wow! Is it that time already? My how the year flies.

                    JAKE
Not me. Him!

MARCUS pulls a quizzical face like I think something sexy is going on here.

                    MARCUS

Oh?!?!

                    ROB
What's that face supposed to mean?

                    MARCUS
Oh, nothing?!?!

MARCUS makes the same face again.

> What time do you make it?

> **JAKE**
> A little after two.

> **MARCUS**
> Rob, what time are we meeting to get the Valentine's stuff?

> **ROB**
> About 5.30 after Lacey finishes work

> **MARCUS**
> Ooh, better hurry.

MARCUS begins to walk ahead of ROB and JAKE then makes a complete turn and walks off back in the direction from which he was originally coming from.

> **JAKE**
> Hey Eric, Rob's seeing a forty-two-year-old woman!

MARCUS looks surprised, then he takes a double-take which causes him to trip off the pavement and straight into an oncoming car. ROB & JAKE stare in disbelief.

                    ROB
        I bet that's going to hurt.

                    JAKE
        Are Afghan coats back in? Coz I didn't get that memo.

After a long pause ROB and JAKE start to walk down the street.

        So, ...do forty-two year olds move around a lot during sex?

4   INT.   A CARD SHOP - DAY   4

LACEY, ROB, JAKE and MARCUS enter a card shop with a big Valentine's Day promotion on.

MARCUS
Time for the annual Valentine's day mashup?

ROB
It's not a mashup.

MARCUS
Oh, I beg to differ Rob. This is definitely a mixture or fusion of disparate elements. I'm certainly a desperado!

ROB
Right, okay, whatever. Now this year guys, no spending hours choosing a Valentine's card let's all go in and choose the first card we like, okay?

JAKE & LACEY
Okay.

ROB
Marcus?

>   **MARCUS**
> Lets rock 'n' roll.

All four of the gang split up and start browsing the cards.

>   **JAKE**
> You know, I'm getting a little bit tired of pretending I'm excited every time it's Valentine's Day. I think they should pass a law where couples only have to celebrate their first Valentine's Day, otherwise every year over and over again you have to come up with the "love" goods.

>   **ROB**
> "Love goods?!?!" There's no answer to that.

JAKE walks off. ROB walks up to MARCUS

> Marcus, decided what you're getting your girlfriend for Valentine's day?

MARCUS
Well, she told me about a week ago that she needs a new pedal bin for the kitchen.

ROB
You haven't?

A broad smile appears on MARCUS' FACE.

You have.

MARCUS
You better believe it Rob! State of the art, top of the range. It even has a built-in sensor that sees you coming and pops up the lid. Boy, will she love it, and to think I usually have trouble getting the right thing for Valentine's Day.

ROB
I think you're going to find out that this wasn't the something she wanted for Valentine's Day.

ROB picks up a card, it is the first one's he's looked at, he has a quick look inside.

Right, that's me sorted. Let's go.

LACEY comes around the corner laughing at the humorous card she has chosen.

LACEY
I've got mine.

LACEY shows the card she has chosen to ROB.

ROB
Really!?!?!

LACEY
Do you get it?

ROB
Of course I get it, but will Simon get it?

LACEY
Don't you think it's funny.

ROB
No.

ROB walks off. LACEY looks perplexed then reads the card again and once again laughs out loud.

JAKE approaches ROB. He has two completely different styles of Valentine Day cards in his hands.

          ROB
Here we go.

          JAKE
I don't know whether to go with funny or romantic?

          ROB
Well, what are you going to give her for a gift?

          JAKE
Hmm, not sure?

          ROB
What about some jewellery? Girls, always like jewellery.

JAKE
No, no. I have to be very careful what I give her as a present. I don't want to send the wrong message. Especially after the cinema incident.

ROB
What if her ex-boyfriend gives her some jewellery?

JAKE
No, no, he can't get her anything more expensive than me. I have to spend at least double what he spends.

ROB
So if he does give her jewellery, what are you going to get her?

JAKE
I don't know. Maybe a Jet Ski!

ROB
A Jet Ski?!?!?

JAKE

You don't understand Rob. My relationship is in a very delicate place. Whatever I give her, she's going to be bringing in relationship experts from all over Britain to interpret the meaning behind it.

ROB

Look forget the Jet Ski. What does she need? Maybe there's something special that she would like you to give her for her house?

JAKE

I think I heard her say something about a Gazebo.

ROB

A Gazebo? Who's ever given someone a Gazebo for Valentine's Day?

JAKE

I don't know, but she's definitely mentioned a Gazebo. Perhaps I'll be the first.

ROB
Who puts a Gazebo in their house?!?!

JAKE walks off, ROB shouts after him.

Look, forget the Gazebo!

MARCUS is in another part of the card shop

MARCUS
Ahh haa! There's the one for me.

MARCUS then proceeds to scramble up one of the card display units to reach a large padded card near the ceiling. He leaves in his wake a pile of dislodged valentine's cards.

MARCUS then proceeds to where LACEY is standing in the "sorry" card section. Then with a little squeaky sound MARCUS breaks wind.

A few seconds later, an OLD LADY starts to sniff the air.

OLD LADY
Oh, my dear lord, what is that smell?

MARCUS hands her a "Sorry" card. A few seconds later LACEY hands her a card with deepest sympathy on.

Meanwhile in another part of the shop.....

JAKE puts the card he wants down next to ROB and goes to put back the card he no longer wants in the correct section. Meanwhile the sweet OLD LADY comes by and picks up JAKE's discarded card and takes an instant liking to it. She heads towards the till. JAKE returns and can't find his card.

JAKE
Rob, where's my card?

ROB
I don't know, where did you put it?

JAKE
Right there, I distinctly remember asking you to look after it for me as it was the last one.

> **ROB**
> You did not.

> **JAKE**
> I did, I did! I'm telling you.

LACEY approaches.

> **LACEY**
> Hey, hasn't that old lady got your card?

JAKE immediately notices the OLD LADY going to pay for her card.

> **JAKE**
> Not for much longer she hasn't. Hey you?

JAKE runs up to the OLD LADY at the queue for the till and addresses her.

>> Uh, excuse me. I know this is going to sound wacky, like something out of a BBC situation comedy, but I, really have to have that card. It's a long story, but my whole future happiness may depend on it.

OLD LADY
Well, I'm sorry young man but I've chosen this card specially to celebrate mine and my husband's 50th Valentine's Day together.

LACEY: turns to ROB who is also watching events unfold and mouths, "ahhhhh!" as she gives ROB a romantic nudge.

JAKE
Yes, well, be that as it may, if you could just find it in yourself to give it up.

OLD LADY
Do you not understand? You're not getting this card.

JAKE
All right. All right! I'll tell you what I'm prepared to do, I will give you double what you're going to pay for it.

OLD LADY
You're in my way young man! Stop hassling me?

The OLD LADY tries to get past JAKE but he now stands in front of her in a confrontational way.

>   **JAKE**
> Give me that card!

>   **OLD LADY**
> Stop it!

>   **JAKE**
> I want that card, lady.

>   **OLD LADY**
> Help! Someone please! Help!

>   **JAKE**
> Shut up, you old cow.

JAKE grabs the card and with an evil laugh runs off out of the shop and down the street.

>   **OLD LADY**
> Stop thief! That man's stolen my
> Valentine's card!

LACEY and ROB just stare in disbelief as events unfold. ROB speaks but to no-one in particular.

                ROB
        I bought a newspaper with cash today.

               LACEY
          (not really listening)
Oh?

                ROB
        That's how they used to do it in World
        War II you know.

LACEY does not react immediately, there is a short pause, then LACEY realises what ROB said makes no sense.

               LACEY
What?!?!

5   INT.   MARCUS' HIPPY FLAT - EVENING   5

ROB, MARCUS and LACEY and their respective partners have met up at MARCUS' hippy flat.

GRAMS: White Rabbit by Jefferson Airplane is playing in the background.

> **LACEY**
> You know, this is the first time I've been to Marcus' flat.

> **ROB**
> Yeah, it's a, somewhat of an acquired taste.

MARCUS enters dressed like an Aztec holy man.

> **MARCUS**
> Greetings friends, and your respective lovers. And welcome to our Valentine's evening exchange ……..thing! ……Ahh, no Jake I see.

> **ROB**
> No, he is still helping the Police with their, Help The Elderly enquires.

MARCUS addresses his girlfriend HONEYBUN in a trying to impress her type of way.

> **MARCUS**
> You know, whenever a Policeman asks me, "if I know why they pulled me over?" I smile, take their hand in mine and say, "Sounds like somebody needs a hug?"

MARCUS makes a bizarre romantic grin towards HONEYBUN.

> **ROB**
> Yeah right, get on with it.

> **MARCUS**
> Okay. Well, let us proceed, and let us all pleasure the ancient God of young lovers on this St Valentine's most sacred of holy days. Let the exchange of presents begin.

MARCUS claps his hands in a dramatic fashion.

LACEY goes first. Her boyfriend SIMON opens his card, he does not find it funny, ROB and LACEY exchange looks with ROB implying told you so. SIMON opens his present, he is even less impressed by it.

>   **SIMON**
> I don't like this present Lacey. You've put zero thought into this.

>   **LACEY**
>   **(Quizzically)**
> Ooh? Hummm sorry. Uh, where's mine?

>   **SIMON**
> Sorry Lacey, but I do not believe in the exchanging of gifts. That is why I have adopted a llama in your name.

>   **MARCUS**
> Nice! Now ROB, would you like to do the honours?

ROB addresses his girlfriend VICKY.

ROB
Maybe you won't like it?

VICKY
Oh, how could I not like it? Of course, I will like it.

ROB
You could 'not' like it.

VICKY
Just the fact that you are giving me a Valentine's card means everything to me.

MARCUS
Rob, if you would like to hand over the card and present now.

ROB
Oh, the card.

He hands VICKY the card.

MARCUS
...And the present Robert!

ROB
The present is inside the card, thank you Marcus.

VICKY
A Dorothy Perkins gift card?!?! You gave me a Dorothy Perkins gift card as a Valentine's Day present?

VICKY is not impressed.

ROB
Well I couldn't think what to get you.

VICKY
Who are you, my grandmother?

MARCUS examines the gift card.

MARCUS
Oh, come on Vicky. There's £78 and 75p there! I don't think that's anything to sneeze at.

MARCUS mouths quizzically "75p" to ROB.

MARCUS' girlfriend HONEYBUN speaks in a weird Eastern European non-defined language.

HONEYBUN
(speaks in a weird Eastern European non-defined language)

MARCUS
Stay right there Honeybun. I'm coming straight back.

HONEYBUN
(speaks in a weird Eastern European non-defined language)

MARCUS
Yes! I have got you something!

HONEYBUN
(speaks in a weird Eastern European non-defined language)

MARCUS
Yeah. Open it baby.

HONEYBUN
(speaks in a weird Eastern European non-defined language as she opens the present. Then as she rips off the last piece of paper she exclaims in English)

Pedal bin!

MARCUS
Yes, I got you the one you wanted. Your kitchen is now complete.

ROB looks both surprised and irritated.

HONEYBUN takes MARCUS on a celebratory dance around the room. MARCUS speaks to ROB as he dances past.

MARCUS
I don't understand women, hey Rob??

ROB
Oh, for Pete's sake, I give up.

HONEYBUN and MARCUS dance till the scene ends.

6   INT.   POLICE STATION - DAY   6

ROB, MARCUS & LACEY are at the police station to pick JAKE up.

ROB
How far did he get this time?

POLICEMAN
Boots the chemist.

MARCUS
Oooh, not bad for Jake.

POLICEMAN
Yeah, a couple of the Specials have been speculating that Jake must be secretly working out.

LACEY
Are you going to charge him?

POLICEMAN
No, as soon as we gave the Valentine's card back to Mrs Voldemort she was quite happy to drop all charges - as long as Jake agreed to do some form of community service as a recompense.

ROB
And don't tell me, it just conveniently happens to coincide with another of your charity shows for HM Prison Knokford?

POLICEMAN
This is so true.

JAKE enters from the cells.

ROB
Well, I hope you're satisfied.

JAKE
I take it's the usual.

LACEY embarrassed looks down at her feet.

LACEY
Of course.

JAKE approaches and addresses MARCUS.

JAKE
Are you okay with this?

MARCUS
What, are you kidding? I love to perform baby, and with a little bit of luck we should nail it this time.

JAKE
I hope so. I do hope so.

>   **ROB**
> Those convicts can be a tough crowd.

ROB, JAKE, MARCUS & LACEY slowly exit the police station.

7   INT.   PRISON DRILL HALL - DAY   7

ROB, JAKE LACEY and MARCUS performing in a live show for the inmates of H.M Prison Knockford.

They are performing their version of "I Am A Fine Musician!"

The inmates are falling about in hysterics.

The POLICEMAN addresses the prison warden.

>   **POLICEMAN**
> Now that has got to be way better than
> the death penalty.

8   EXT.   A HIGH STREET - DAY   8

ROB and JAKE are walking down the street. JAKE suddenly stops abruptly.

> **JAKE**
> A Dorothy Perkins gift card? You got to be kidding me. What kind of gift is that? That's like something her grandmother would give her.

THE END.

Printed in Great Britain
by Amazon